GET A GRIP, VIVY COHEN!

Sarah Kapit

Dial Books for Young Readers

Dial Books for Young Readers
An imprint of Penguin Random House LLC, New York

First published in the United States of America by Dial Books for Young Readers, 2020
First paperback edition published 2021

Puffin Books & colophon are registered trademarks of Penguin Books Limited.

Visit us online at penguinrandomhouse.com.

THE LIBRARY OF CONGRESS HAS CATALOGED THE HARDCOVER EDITION AS FOLLOWS:
Names: Kapit, Sarah, author. Title: Get a grip, Vivy Cohen! / Sarah Kapit.
Description: New York : Dial Books for Young Readers, [2020] | Summary: Eleven-year-old
knuckleball pitcher Vivy Cohen, who has autism, becomes pen pals with her favorite Major
League baseball player after writing a letter to him as an assignment for her social skills class.
Identifiers: LCCN 2019018644 | ISBN 9780525554189 (hardcover)
Subjects: | CYAC: Baseball—Fiction. | Autism—Fiction. | Pen pals—Fiction. | Letters—
Fiction. | Family life—Fiction. Classification: LCC PZ7.1.K32 Get 2020 | DDC [Fic]—dc23
Printed in the United States of America

ISBN 9780525554196

5th Printing

Design by Cerise Steel
Text set in Chaparral Pro

GET A GRIP,
VIVY COHEN!

To all advocates of neurodiversity,
past, present, and future.

Dear Vincent James Capello,

Hi! I'm Vivian Jane Cohen—VJC, just like you. That's a sign of a connection between us, isn't it? I think so. But I don't go by VJ like you do. People just call me Vivy.

Well, that's not really important. The really important thing is this: I want to be a knuckleball pitcher when I grow up. Just like you. My mom says that's impossible because there's never been a girl in the major leagues. Still, someone has to be first, right? And I'd like it to be me.

I don't know if it's actually possible, but my brother, Nate, says I throw a wicked knuckleball. He's on the varsity team as a catcher even though he's only a freshman in high school! That's really impressive, don't you think? So if Nate says my knuckleball is good, then it must be at least a little bit true.

The problem is, I've never pitched in a real game. I don't play for a team. And I don't know if I ever will.

But that's not a very happy subject to write about, and I want this letter to be happy. So now I'm going to talk about something else.

I bet you're wondering why I'm writing to you, out of all the bajillions of people in the world. Well, besides your general awesomeness, we actually know each other. Sort of. I met you three years ago, when you were still pitching in the minors. You probably don't remember, but for me, well, it was the most important day ever!

Here's what happened. My family and I went to a California Tornados game for this social thingy with the Autism Foundation. I didn't like the game—loud and boring, which means, not for me. The seat felt so sticky against my skin. I bounced up and down even though Mom kept telling me, "Sit still, Vivy!"

Then we went into the clubhouse to meet the players.

You weren't like the others. They talked to us in loud voices, which was pretty stupid because being autistic doesn't mean you can't hear anything. They used that funny voice teachers do sometimes, the one that needs to explaaain thiinnggs veeeeerrry sloooowllly. Not you.

You saw me wandering around in the back corner and came up to me with a big smile on your face. You tried talking to me, but I don't talk to strangers.

I fought very, very hard against the urge to run. I wanted so much to get back to my own room, away from all the strangers and their big voices and stinky armpits.

That's when you pulled out a baseball and showed me your knuckleball grip—four fingers clenched into a fist.

"The knuckleball is a very special pitch," you said. "It completely defies the laws of physics because it doesn't spin in the air like other pitches. Try it."

I didn't understand much about physics and stuff, but I liked the idea of throwing a super-special pitch. Except I didn't think it would be a very good idea to throw a baseball with all those people right there. "Now?" I asked.

You laughed. "Not in the clubhouse! But when you get home, will you give it a try?"

"Yes," I said.

You smiled. "I think you'll like it."

When I went home that night, I tried throwing the knuckleball for real. The first two pitches bounced into the grass. Then the third pitch sailed right over the backyard fence, so I lost the ball forever. Nate got really mad at me, because I borrowed it from him without asking. Oops. After that I asked Mom and Dad for my very own baseball. Even though it was hard, I knew I wanted to learn the pitch that defies the laws of physics. Your pitch.

Every day since then, I've practiced throwing the knuckleball. I'm not sure how many days that is, but it must be an awful lot. I can also throw a two-seam fastball, though it isn't exactly fast. But I guess no one says they throw a two-seam sort-of-but-not-really-fastball. Even if it is closer to the truth.

I wish so much I could pitch for a real team. Like in that movie where girls played baseball because all the boys were off fighting in World War II and stuff. But all that happened a really long time ago. In real life, girls don't play baseball. Especially not autistic ones. I've asked about it a million and three times, but Mom keeps saying I should play softball instead. No matter how many times I explain everything to her, she doesn't understand that it's harder to throw a knuckleball with a great big softball.

And if I can't throw the knuckleball, I don't want to play.

I'm writing to you because I need to write a letter to someone for my social skills group and I chose you. My dad says it's okay. He's a big fan of yours too.

To be completely honest, I don't understand the point of this assignment because everyone in the whole world uses email. DUH. But when I mentioned this fact to Sandra, the counselor who runs the group, she just let out a sound that sounded very not-nice to my ears. "Just do what you're told, Vivy," she said.

Adults sure like saying that, don't they? And I want to be good, so I am doing what I'm told. Even though I don't entirely understand why I'm doing it.

Oh, sorry. You're probably not very interested in Sandra. Since you're a super-famous pitcher and all. I mean, you've been an All-Star twice, plus you won the Cy Young Award! You probably don't have time to read letters from eleven-year-old girls at all. But I wanted to try anyway. It took a really long time for me to find an address on the official team website. Someone should fix that, in my opinion. But I did find it and now I'm sending you a letter. Since we've met before, we're not strangers.

Also, pitchers and catchers report to spring training today and I wanted to wish you good luck. Not that YOU of all people need luck, of course, but I figured you're probably pretty down after what happened in the World Series last year. That must have been really hard. I know what it's like to mess things up.

I wanted to tell you that even after what happened, you still have lots of fans like me who are rooting for you. My dad says it's our year, and I think he's right.

Sincerely,
Vivian Jane Cohen, also known as Vivy

P.S. Do you know why the knuckleball is called a knuckleball when you don't actually use your knuckles to throw it? Wouldn't it make more sense to call it a fingertipball?

Dear VJ,

Is it okay if I call you VJ? I know it would be proper manners to call you Mr. Capello, but all the TV announcers call you VJ, so that's how I think of you.

You're probably surprised to hear from me again. I was only supposed to write one letter for social skills group, but I liked it so much I thought I'd write another one, just to say hi. I like writing letters to you for some reason. And I found a big stack of envelopes and stamps in the kitchen, so I figured, well, why not?

You didn't write back to me, but that's totally okay. I know you must be busy in spring training. Mom and Dad say that if I'm good maybe we'll get tickets for a game this year. Of course, I really want it to be a game where you pitch, but any game will be exciting. I'm much more grown-up now than I was three years ago. Now I understand baseball.

Also, I really don't want to bother you or anything, but something's been bugging me. It's about baseball, so I thought maybe you could help.

Well, actually, some ONE has been bugging me: Nate. I used to throw with him all the time, but now he won't play baseball with me anymore! The other day I went into his room to see if he wanted to throw a ball around in the backyard.

I found Nate sprawled out on his bed. And let me tell you, that bed was totally NOT made in the way Mom likes. The walls of his room were covered in posters of baseball players—mostly all the super-great catchers like Buster Posey and Gary Sánchez. Except for this one picture of a dark-haired pitcher I didn't recognize.

The moment I entered, Nate twisted his face all funny and slammed his laptop shut. "You know, there's this thing called knocking," he said in his grumpy voice. "You might want to try it sometime. Works great."

I know you're probably wondering how I managed to remember everything he said so well. The answer is that I just keep thinking about what happened. What I could have done better. So I really do remember every single thing he said. Maybe one or two words aren't completely right, but that doesn't matter. The point is, he was being mean.

"I know what knocking is," I told him, because duh. "But I wanted to know if you can do a throwing session with me."

Nate glared at me so hard that I could feel my spine shrink in. "I'm not your personal catcher, Vivy. I have my own life and it's kind of important. Not that anyone around here gives a flying Triceratops about that."

Actually, he did not say "flying Triceratops." I can't repeat his actual word because it was very bad and I am not going to use a bad word in my letter to you. I changed it to "flying Triceratops" because it's such a funny expression. Dad says it sometimes.

"I care about your life," I insisted. "But when DO you want to play with me?"

Maybe it was stupid to keep talking when he was obviously in a super-bad mood, but VJ, I just didn't understand why he was acting like this! I know he's busy with baseball, but Nate always throws with me at least once a week. And we haven't done it in ten whole days. Which is basically forever in pitcher-time. So obviously we needed to do it again soon. Right?

Nate gave me another grumpy monster-glare. "When I feel like playing catch with you, I'll let you know, okay? But right now I'm busy and I just can't."

The way he said "playing catch" . . . VJ, I'm not exactly

sure how to describe it, but there was just something in his voice that I didn't like. I always thought our throwing sessions were more important than just playing catch, you know? But I guess he doesn't agree.

"Okay," I whispered. I could feel an awful prickly feeling swell up in my eyes, so I had to get out of there. Before I did something really, really stupid.

VJ, why would my brother act like this? He never used to be mean! Did I do something wrong? I say the wrong thing a lot, even when I don't mean to, so maybe that's what happened. What do you think? You can give me your honest opinion. I promise.

Sincerely,
Vivy

Dear VJ,

Oh my gosh, VJ, I have GOT to tell you about everything that just happened. I can't talk to anyone else about it right now and it's just so amazing and . . . anyway, I'll try to explain.

I told you before about how weird Nate's being and how he never wants to play with me anymore. It's very confusing. I know he's a high school student and a varsity catcher and all, but how can he be too busy for ME, his sister? Does he not want to spend time with me anymore? (I've been wondering: Do you have any siblings, VJ? I bet they always want to play ball with you.)

But today Nate said we could go to Crescent Memorial Park and throw together. FINALLY! You probably don't know much about Lakeview, California, but Crescent Memorial is the biggest park we have. There are two whole baseball diamonds, but during the season they're usually full. That doesn't leave much pitching time for knuckle-ballers who don't have a team.

Since it was gray and chilly out, there weren't many people at the park—good news for me! I'm certainly not going to let a few clouds keep me from pitching. You wouldn't. I remember that one game when there was lightning and stuff but you still threw a shutout.

Today Nate was totally being Nice Helpful Older Brother Nate, not Grumpy Nate Who Always Says No. If you ask me, it's weird that he acts so different one day as compared to the next. I hope this means Nate's grouchiness is over for good!

Nate says the pitcher's mound at the park is set to youth baseball standards. I guess that means it's shorter than the mound you throw on, but every time I get up there I'm still amazed by how tall I become. The extra height makes me feel just a little braver.

I threw to him for about half an hour. My first fifteen pitches were all way outside the strike zone, but then Nate came over to give me some tips. He knows a lot about pitching because he used to be a pitcher himself. He taught me my delivery and everything. A few years ago, he switched to playing catcher because pitching hurts his arm too much. Personally, I think sitting crouched behind the plate all game long looks way worse than throwing a few pitches, but it's nice for me that he can catch. He's even good at catching the knuckleball.

"You have to imagine the target in your mind," he said. "Like a big red X. Then you throw to the mark every time."

I started to imagine giant red Xs floating around in the strike zone, and then the knuckleball came to me. It zigged and zagged all over the place. Just like a good knuckleball should.

That's when the most amazing thing happened. After about thirty pitches, a tall man came up and started watching us. He had been throwing with his son out on the field, but he left to watch me. Can you believe that, VJ?

For about ten pitches, he just watched me from the sidelines. I had to try really, really hard to concentrate on pitching. I'm sure you probably don't care about people watching you, but for me it was all so new. And kind of scary.

Finally, the man spoke. "You!" he said without smiling. "Where'd you learn how to throw that knuckleball?"

Like I said before, I don't talk to strangers. But since he asked me a direct question, I knew I should answer. I looked over at Nate and he nodded.

So I said, "VJ Capello."

He laughed really, really hard at that. I don't think he

believed me. Even though it's 100% true: You taught me the grip.

"I think I like you, kid," he said. "Hey, you ever use that knuckle in a game?"

"She's not into softball," Nate explained for me. He stepped closer to me while the man asked all those questions. He even put a hand on my shoulder.

"Got it," the man said. "You can't throw a real knuckleball with a softball, especially not with those small hands. But I bet you could fool batters with that knuckle in a baseball game."

Pitch in a baseball game! Me!

I knew right then that this was a Very Important Moment.

But Nate just didn't get the important-ness of everything. "Um, what?" he said.

"I coach a team in the Apricot League," the man said. "And we could always use pitchers. You look like you're around eleven, right? That's perfect for my team."

People always say "my heart skipped a beat" and I never know what that even means because how can your heart ACTUALLY skip a beat? But right then I swear that my heart really did skip. I started flapping my hands like crazy, even though my therapists always say not to. It's hard to explain to people, but I guess I just needed to feel my hands flick up and down. The man's stern face didn't change one bit.

I don't usually pay much attention to faces, but I tried to remember a few things about this man: Brown hair, graying around the edges. A lined and pale-ish white face that looked very serious, but maybe also kind.

"But she's a girl," Nate said.

"That's sexist!" I told him. Really, I expect better from my brother.

The man pulled his shoulders up. "Yeah, I can see she's a girl. So what? You ever hear of Mo'ne Davis? 2014 Little League World Series, she goes out and throws a shutout. Or how about Eri Yoshida? She's a knuckleballer too. Played pro in the Japanese leagues."

I flapped harder and carefully placed those names in my memory, so I could look them up later. Mo'ne Davis and Eri Yoshida: my new heroes. Along with you, VJ, of course.

It's weird, but it didn't occur to me before that there could be other girls playing baseball right now. But of course there are, and that made me want to play more than ever. Who knows? Maybe someday people will talk about Mo'ne Davis, Eri Yoshida, and Vivy Cohen.

"Um. It's not just the girl thing," Nate said. He shot me

a look and mouthed a word that looked an awful lot like "sorry." "My sister, she has special needs. I don't know if my parents will be okay with her playing baseball."

I could feel all my hope go POOF the moment he said "special needs." Nate was right, of course. I just knew the man would walk away, saying obviously he'd made a mistake. No special needs girls for his team.

Only he didn't. "The only special I care about is that knuckleball," he said. "Now that is something special. Hey, why don't we ask her what she thinks? Would you like to be on my team, kid?"

"Yes," I said. I didn't need to think about it.

He finally smiled a little. "I thought so. Now why don't you go talk to your family about it? You don't need to decide anything right away."

Then he scribbled something on a piece of paper and handed it to Nate. "Call me after you've talked to your folks," he said.

By now his son had wandered over to us and I realized I know him from school. He's a grade ahead of me and his name is Chris or Kevin or something. I don't know. I'm not good with faces and I've never cared about the seventh-grade boys at all. Since I'm in sixth grade, there's really no reason for me to talk with them, ever.

"What are you doing?" the boy whined. "We have to work on my curve!"

"Patience, boy," the coach told him. "I'm recruiting for the team."

"HER?"

I suddenly felt hot all over and I really, really wanted to break my no-talking-to-strangers rule to tell off Chris or Kevin or whoever he was. But the coach did the telling-off for me. "Yes, HER," he said. "Now zip it or beat it."

I guess it was pretty mean for the man to say that to his own kid, but the boy WAS being horrible. I liked this stranger-man more and more.

The terrible boy gave me a really nasty look, but he wasn't stupid enough to say anything else in front of his dad. I noticed that the boy and coach had the same square jaw and dark eyes. Except somehow it looked ugly on the boy.

"Think it over," the coach said to me. "We could use your knuckle for sure."

"I have a question," I blurted out, just as the coach began turning away.

"Sure, kid."

"What's your name?" I asked. I wanted to know so he wouldn't be a stranger.

"Call me Coach K," he said.

Coach K—K for strikeout! Isn't that great? It's one of those things that just feels right, like you and me having the same initials. I flapped quietly while Coach K and the awful boy left.

"Do you think I can be a real pitcher?" I asked Nate. I figured that if anyone would know, it'd be him. I hoped so much he would say yes, but I wasn't at all sure.

"Yeah, I do. But Mom and Dad might need some convincing."

Oh, right. Them.

I flapped my fingers so hard they started to ache.

So . . . I haven't told my parents what happened, even though we left the park more than five hours ago. I just can't do it yet. Maybe by the time you get this letter I'll work up the nerve. Then again, maybe not.

I'm extra-worried about Mom. She has a lot of funny ideas about what I should do. And what I shouldn't. Back in elementary school she wanted me to stay in special ed even though it was the most boring thing ever. And then she wasn't sure about me going to Hebrew school for some weird reason. Eventually she gave in when our rabbi started a special program for autistic kids. It's not that I mind doing stuff with other autistic kids—I don't!—but I don't know why she thinks I can ONLY do things that are For Autistic Children.

So I need to be very, very careful when I tell her about Coach K and baseball. It has to be 100% perfect, not like that time a few months ago when I asked Mom if I could quit social skills group and she said, "Absolutely not, now finish your cauliflower."

I don't know if they'll let me join the team.

But VJ, I want it so much.

Sincerely,
Vivy

Dear VJ,

It's not going to happen. I hate everything.

Vivy

Dear VJ,

My last letter didn't explain things very well. I thought I would write again to tell you exactly what happened. Just in case you happen to be interested, which you probably aren't.

The day after I met Coach K, Nate and I sat down for a Very Important Talk with my parents. Nate suggested it. (Yes, I know it's not grammatically correct to capitalize things like that, but I feel like the capital letters show how super-important the talk really was. Plain old regular letters just aren't enough sometimes.)

I'm really glad that Nate decided to help me. Maybe he's back to being nice Nate 100% of the time. That would be so great, wouldn't it?

Nate's a much better talker than me, so I let him do most of the talking. "I've got this," Nate told me before we went in. "You're going to be pitching in real games soon, just wait."

But when Nate finished explaining everything that

happened at the park, Mom just stared into empty space for a really long time. My palms started to sweat—very gross! I looked at Dad. He's on my side, probably, but he won't say so. Not until after Mom said her thing—whatever that is.

I waited for a bajillion years. (Okay, so it wasn't actually a bajillion. Obviously. But it sure felt like a long time.)

Finally, Mom spoke. "I hate to say it, but I really don't know about all this. I just don't think it'll be good for Vivy."

"Why not?" Nate asked. "You're always saying Vivy should get more involved in extracurricular activities and stuff. Playing baseball would be awesome for her."

My brother is annoying sometimes—well, a lot of the time. But I love him so much. I really do.

Mom sighed. "Yes, I know. But baseball . . . that's a boy's sport. It's dangerous. She's so young and small and I'm just not sure it's right for her. Why not play softball instead?"

"You can't throw a knuckleball with a softball!" I told her.

That's actually a little bit of a lie. You can throw a knuckleball with a softball, but it's way harder. I don't want to bother learning that when I still need to perfect my REAL knuckleball. I didn't tell Mom, though. She doesn't know the difference between a knuckleball and a split-fingered fastball, so there's no use trying to explain baseball stuff to her.

Besides, it never matters what I say.

Mom's frown got bigger and I could tell she was Very Unhappy. "Honey, is it really so important for you to do this knuckleball thing? Can't you play without it?"

"No," I said.

She turned to Dad, who'd been very quiet through this whole thing. "See, this is the problem," she said. "The whole knuckleball issue seems like a fixation, and the therapists are very clear on this. We shouldn't be encouraging her fixations."

I hate hate HATE when she does this. I'm right there and she talks about me like I can't hear it! And I especially hate when she calls my knuckleball a "fixation."

No matter what she says, my knuckleball isn't some silly thing that little kids do, like when I was younger and carried my stuffed panda Lolly around everywhere. I've worked so hard on my knuckleball and a real live coach thinks I can pitch. Doesn't that mean something, anything?

I bet no one ever told you that you couldn't play.

The problem is that Mom doesn't care about baseball, if you can believe it. She's always complaining about how Dad watches baseball all the time. She doesn't get what it's like to be totally sucked in by a game, to sit on the edge of your seat with every ball and strike. And she definitely doesn't understand that feeling of wonderfulness that comes over me when the ball hits the catcher's mitt with a loud SMACK.

You understand. I've seen you talk about it in your post-game interviews. (I always, ALWAYS watch the postgame interview for your starts.)

Dad kept quiet through all this, which was kind of annoying, to be honest. I know baseball is super-important to him because he always says that he has two religions—Reform Judaism and baseball. So obviously he should want me to play. But he let Mom talk first.

Then he spoke. FINALLY. He took off his glasses and fiddled with them while he talked. "Rachel, I know you're worried. But this could be good for Vivy," he said. "It's a chance for her to make friends. I think we should consider it."

A tiny bit of hope returned to me. Maybe this could work out after all. Maybe, maybe, maybe! It's better than a no.

Mom's face did all sorts of twisty things. I don't always know exactly what her faces mean, but I'm pretty sure this meant she was thinking about it.

"I just don't know," she said finally. "There's so much that can happen out there. I really think we should talk to Dr. Reeve about this before we make any big decisions."

Even though Mom didn't say absolutely not, talking to Dr. Reeve probably means no. She's my therapist. If I want something, she says no most of the time. This isn't going to be any different. I know it.

Personally I think it's all very unfair that Mom still treats me like a baby even though I'm going to be twelve in just five months. Twelve is a very grown-up age, AND it's only one year away from thirteen, which is very important because when I turn thirteen I'm going to have my bat mitzvah. That means I'll be an Official Adult according to Jewish law (even if I still won't be able to drive and all of that). But Mom sure doesn't act like I'm going to be a sort-of-adult soon, does she?

So ever since the Talk, I've been playing it over again and again in my head. Wondering if maybe there was something I could have done differently. But I can't think of a single thing that would have convinced Mom.

I shouldn't have hoped for anything. Coach K was just so cool and nice that I thought maybe . . .

At least your baseball season starts soon. Six weeks to Opening Day! I bet you're super-excited, right? I sure am. I know you're going to do great.

I just . . . well, I just really wish I had my own Opening Day.

From,
Vivy

Dear VJ,

I'm meeting with Dr. Reeve today. Wish me luck!

Vivy

Dear VJ,

Yesterday I had my appointment with Dr. Reeve. I don't know if you've ever been to therapy, but I'm guessing probably not. So I'm going to explain it to you.

My mom takes me to appointments, but she usually waits outside while I talk to Dr. Reeve. Sometimes she comes in, but usually that is a Very Bad Thing.

Anyway, the appointment began like usual. Dr. Reeve asked me a bunch of questions about how things are going at school, at home, blah blah blah. I showed her my behavior chart, which proved that I had absolutely no meltdowns in the past week. I think that's pretty good, don't you?

"So your mother tells me you want to play baseball," she said. "Let's talk about this. Why baseball? Why not softball?"

I wanted to scream at the top of my lungs, but I knew if I did she'd never let me play. VJ, why do people keep saying that girls should play softball and ONLY softball? It's not like being a girl means I can't throw or hit a baseball! (Actually, I am bad at hitting, but I don't think it's because I'm a girl. That would be like saying I'm a bad hitter because I have brown hair. It's just stupid!)

If I were smarter, I would have told Dr. Reeve all this. But I didn't.

Instead, I took a few deep breaths and tried to explain to her about the knuckleball and how it works and stuff. I even pulled out the baseball I keep in my backpack to show her the knuckleball grip.

"Hmm," she said after I finished. "I see."

What does that even mean, she sees? What did she see? I wanted to ask her, but I knew I needed to be 100% good. I did my best to look her in the eyes when I talked with her. To show her I deserve to pitch.

Like always, she had loads more questions. "I know the knuckleball is important to you, but don't you think you'd like to play with other girls?"

"I see other girls at school," I said. I didn't mention that they're not exactly my friends, though Dr. Reeve probably knows that already. "Why can't I play with boys? It's mostly boys at social skills group, and you make me go there."

Her lips twitched and I got the terrible feeling that

somehow I'd messed up. Because of course I'd mess up and say something stupid at a time like this.

That's when Dr. Reeve shooed me from the room. "Thank you for sharing your feelings. Now I need to talk with your mother. Okay?"

I could only hope I hadn't completely blown my chance. You say that great pitchers always make the most of their opportunities. Did I do that? I wasn't sure.

There was no one else in the waiting room. Just the boring old goldfish in the tank.

I knew I shouldn't, but I crept up to the office door and listened in. I couldn't understand most of what they were saying, but I'm pretty sure Mom said the word "appropriate" at least three times. I don't think I like that word very much. Also, I didn't understand why she kept talking about baseball and whether or not it's APPROPRIATE. Coach K thinks it's appropriate for me to play! Wouldn't he know? Also, I looked it up online and found out that lots of girls play baseball. EIGHTEEN girls have played in the Little League World Series, including my new hero, Mo'ne Davis. I don't know why Mom thinks baseball is INAPPROPRIATE for me.

Dr. Reeve called me into her office. (Luckily, I was back in my seat by then.)

"Maybe you can explain to your mother why you want to play baseball. Like you did with me," Dr. Reeve suggested once I came in again.

I forced myself to look at Mom. Even though I couldn't quite manage to look right into her eyes, I tried for her nose. Hopefully I didn't stare at her too hard, because they don't like it when I do that, either.

"Baseball is fun," I said. "Coach K says I can help the team with my knuckleball. I just . . . I really, really want to play."

That wasn't even close to everything I wanted to say. I wanted to tell Mom about the happy flutter that tickles my stomach when the knuckleball floats in just the right way. I wanted to tell her about meeting you three years ago. How I want to do you proud. It's just hard for me to find the right words sometimes, especially when I have to Make Eye Contact. Ugh, eye contact! It's totally the worst.

I grabbed the squishy orange ball Dr. Reeve keeps in her office. Before I realized it, my fist clenched into my knuckleball grip. I just kept thinking *pleasepleaseplease!* Please let Mom allow me to do this one thing.

Mom grunted and I allowed myself to hope. Just a little bit. "You want to help the team," she repeated.

Hello, didn't I just say that? But I didn't say that out loud because it would be Extremely Rude.

"Well, I don't know. This is quite a step. But I guess we can give it a try," she said.

She said yes!!! She really did!

I got so excited that I could barely keep track of all the things she said next. And I flapped my hands, because if that's not a hand-flapping moment, then what is?

For once, Mom and Dr. Reeve didn't say anything about the flapping. But Mom had plenty of other things to say.

"Of course it all depends on your behavior," she said in her serious voice. "You have to show us that you can handle the stress of playing a sport, Vivy."

Of course. Mom and Dr. Reeve went over a bunch of rules: I go to social skills group every week without complaining, eat my vegetables even when Mom serves really gross ones like yellow squash, and don't have any meltdowns that involve screaming. Plus a whole bunch of other things that will probably be really hard to do.

Right now, I don't care. I'm going to play baseball!

Wish me luck,
Vivy

P.S. Oh my gosh, I just realized what this means. I am going to play in a game. For real. Were you this scared before your first game? Probably not.

Dear VJ,

Great news: I am officially a pitcher for the Lakeview Flying Squirrels!

Yes, our team name is the Flying Squirrels. Please don't laugh. When I asked Coach K about it, he just kind of grunted and made a not-happy face. Okay, so it's not a cool team name like the Giants. But I don't care. The only thing that matters is that I'm on the team. I've got a uniform now and everything. It's bright blue with gray letters that read COHEN across the back. There's also a logo for Mike's Plumbing, the best in Northern California. Or at least that's what it says.

I guess everyone tried out for teams a few weeks ago and stuff, but obviously I didn't because I didn't even know that I could play baseball for real. Coach K said he had to "pull a few strings" with the league so I could join the Flying Squirrels after everyone already picked teams. At first I didn't understand what that meant—did he actually tug strings for me? What color were they? Were they like shoelaces, or twine? But then he explained that he just had to talk with the people in charge and stuff. They said it was okay I didn't go through the usual tryouts since Lakeview is a tiny town. Coach K said our division of the Apricot League is considered non-competitive. Honestly, I don't know what that's even supposed to mean. Everything seems plenty competitive to me!

You probably don't know what the Apricot League is. Until a few days ago, I didn't know either. So I'll tell you. It's sort of like Little League but it's not. We're our own league. Coach K says the Apricot League is very popular in our part of California. Personally, I wish it were called something different. I don't like apricots—they're just so wrinkly. But I guess that's not very important.

Here's a much more important thing: I'm wearing number 49. Just like you! I read once that 49 is traditionally a knuckleballer's number as a tribute to Hoyt Willhelm, who is the most awesome-est knuckleballer ever. I mean, Hoyt kept pitching until he was 49 years old got into the Hall of Fame and everything. Now I get to wear a number that honors him. How great is that?

Something not so great: the boys on my team. Coach K's son is totally the worst—do you remember him? His name is Kyle and he's a pitcher too. I have to admit he's pretty good. He throws a fastball and a curveball and is working on a changeup. No knuckleball, though.

Today was my first practice. When it was time for me to pitch, my whole body trembled so much. That completely threw me off for the first three pitches. They skittered straight into the dirt, at least a foot away from the catcher. It was so embarrassing, VJ. I just KNEW Kyle and the others were thinking "Why is she even here?"

I closed my eyes and tried to forget about all the people and their noise. I tried to remember what it feels like when I throw to Nate. Just him and me in the backyard.

It worked. My next set of pitches was good: almost no rotation, lots of zigging and zagging. I smiled at the catcher, who did a great job. He only missed about half the balls, which for his first time catching the knuckleball is super-amazing.

But when I finished I saw that awful Kyle staring at me with the biggest scowl on his face.

Then he came up to me and spoke. I remember every single mean word.

"Just so you know, I don't care what my dad thinks. You never would have made it through tryouts. You're not even a real pitcher. That pitch is just a lame-o trick. Everyone will figure that out soon enough. And when they do it's bye-bye."

What a horrible jerk. I'd like to see him do it, if he thinks it's so easy!

Now that I'm home and telling you about everything, I realize I should have said that to Kyle. I should have said something smart. But once he started insulting me I just got prickly all over and I couldn't think of the right thing to say.

"You're mean," I told him.

He laughed hysterically, and so did the two other boys who always lurk around him. My face got even hotter underneath my Flying Squirrels cap. I knew I'd made a mistake, but I had no idea how to fix it. Sandra from social skills group always says we should ignore bullies, but how can I possibly ignore Kyle when he tells me I'm not a real pitcher? I couldn't do it, VJ!

"Oh, look. It thinks it can speak to us," one of Kyle's friends said. I think he plays second base, but I haven't learned his name yet. And now I don't want to. While he talked he did this weird squeak with his voice, sort of like a cartoon character.

The boys laughed at me again. My heart thumped so hard I could feel the blood swishing around in my ears. I clutched my old scuffed-up baseball in my hand and kept trying to think of something I could say to make things better. Or maybe just run for it. But those boys are faster than me, and I couldn't convince my feet to budge.

Luckily, Coach K's deep voice cut through their howling. "Fielding drills! Everyone in center field NOW!"

Thank goodness for Coach K!

For the rest of practice I did my very best to keep far away from them. Have you ever met ballplayers like Kyle, VJ? Boys who think you're not good enough? I'm guessing no, because you're such a great pitcher and everything.

I hope the other boys on the team aren't like this. They already know each other, of course. They've played together since they were little kids in T-ball, so I'm the weird one. As usual.

Well, it doesn't matter. I get to play ball. Probably. They wouldn't kick me out after giving me a uniform, right? Even though I didn't try out for the team like everyone else? I mean, Coach K said it didn't matter and he is more important than stupid Kyle. Ugh! I don't even want to think about it right now.

Anyway, Mom is still being weird about me playing baseball. After practice she asked a million questions: Did my arm hurt, were the boys nice to me, and did I really still want to keep playing baseball?

"Of course I do!" I said. Because duh.

Mom didn't say anything, but her lips twitched all funny. Oh well. She can't keep acting like this forever . . . right?

At least Dad is happy for me. Today he said, "You could be the best Jewish pitcher since Sandy Koufax. Maybe even the best ever! Who knows?"

Of course I had to giggle at THAT. I mean, Sandy Koufax was left-handed, more than a foot taller than I am, and threw a wicked curveball. I've tried throwing that pitch and believe me, it does not curve. It is more like a wiggle-ball. But even though Dad was being ridiculous, I kind of loved that he said it. I wonder why he doesn't say that kind of thing to Mom.

From,
Vivy

P.S. I know teammates are supposed to root for each other. Coach K says so. But is it really so wrong for me to hope that Kyle gives up a grand slam?

Dear VJ,

A lot of the time I don't know why I keep writing these letters when you never write back. Not that I'm mad at you or anything. Please don't think that! I just noticed, that's all.

I guess I don't entirely know why I write you these letters, but I usually feel better once I do. So I'm going to keep writing, even if you never write me back.

Plus, there's just so MUCH I have to say. It's not the biggest deal ever or anything, but a Very Cool Thing happened: Mom agreed that I can dress up as Phil Niekro for Purim! (You know, the totally awesome knuckleballer who won 318 games.)

Oh, right. I just realized you might not know what Purim is. It's a Jewish holiday that's sort of like Halloween because we dress up in costumes. Plus there's a play and a carnival. It's a very noisy holiday, which means it's not my favorite. I like carnivals and everything, but can't people be a little quieter about it? Of course, now that I get to dress up as a legendary knuckleballer, I'm looking forward to Purim much more.

Last year Mom made me dress up as Queen Esther. The costume she made for me was really hot and itchy—ugh. Maybe Phil isn't exactly a traditional Purim costume, but I'm way happier to go as him. Dad ordered a jersey for me online that's a replica of the jerseys they wore way back in the 1970s. Isn't that so awesome?

But it's not just my costume that I wanted to talk about. I have to tell you about school. Things are changing, and it's all because of baseball.

Today Kyle the Terrible and his friends found me at lunch. Even though they're in seventh grade and usually don't bother with sixth graders like me.

I was eating at my usual table in the corner of the cafeteria, as far away from the awful loudness as I can possibly get. I used to eat lunch in the hallway, but then a teacher saw me and told me that's against the rules. So I can't do it anymore.

One or two other people sit at my table, but we don't ever talk. One of them is named Bryan and he can't talk. His aide was there with him at lunch, but then Bryan got upset about something and they went away. That left me all alone.

After that, Kyle and his horrible friends came up and sat down right across from me. I wanted to tell them LEAVE

NOW, but I couldn't. I guess there's no actual rule that says they can't sit there. But I didn't like it one bit.

"Why are you here?" I asked them, trying very hard to keep cool. Only sometimes making words is hard for me when I'm nervous, so it all came out like *whyareyouhere* with no spaces in between.

"Really, VIVY, there's no need to be rude. We just wanted to get to know our newest teammate," Kyle said. He smiled at me, but I'm 100% sure it was fake.

I didn't say anything in response to his fakey-ness. (Is that a word? It should be.) At that moment all I wanted was to eat my cheese sandwich. Just so you know, I only like cheese on my sandwich, no ham or roast beef or anything else. I don't understand why people ruin the yumminess of cheese by lumping it in with slimy ham.

Much like ham and cheese, Kyle and peace don't go together. He kept looking at me, his lips curled up in an ugly snarl. My cheeks warmed up and I fumbled with the sandwich. Crumbs got all over my chin and I couldn't brush them away because my hands were full.

Kyle saw my sandwich problem, and his smirk just got wider and uglier. He turned to his big stupid friends. "Oh, great. I thought my father got a regular girl for our team, but it's even worse. We have ourselves a monkey-girl. She can't even eat a sandwich! Or talk like a real person."

He started making noises that I guess were supposed to be monkey sounds. They reminded me more of a cartoon chipmunk. (Not a squirrel. He doesn't deserve to be a squirrel, even if he is officially a Flying Squirrel.)

But even though Kyle stinks at making animal noises, it still hurt. I felt stupid, itchy tears welling up in my eyes. I will not cry, I told myself. I will not cry.

Except . . . I was losing that battle.

That's when another boy walked up to the table. I thought he looked familiar: kind of short with spiky black hair and brown skin. I couldn't quite remember him at first because of my problem with faces.

I did not like this very much. At first I figured he came over to join the let's-make-fun-of-Vivy party. I mean, why else would anyone bother with me?

But then he glared at Kyle and slid into the seat next to mine. So I began to think that maybe everything wasn't completely terrible after all. Still, I didn't really know this boy. And that made me really, really nervous.

"Hi, Vivian!" he said to me. He turned to the other boys with narrowed eyes. "Hey, Kyle. What are you guys doing? I hope you're not trying to bully our new pitcher. I'm sure your dad would be really interested to hear about it if you were. But even you guys wouldn't act like such total losers. Right?"

Kyle glared. "Watch it, Carrillo. Believe me: You don't want to get on my bad side."

Still, he stood up and they left after that. They actually left!

The boy—whose name is Alex Carrillo—smiled at me. Once he started talking I remembered why he's familiar: He's a catcher for the Flying Squirrels. MY catcher.

"Your knuckleball is the coolest pitch ever," he told me. "It's super-hard to catch, but you're like our team's secret weapon. Nobody expects the knuckle."

Talking to a boy who is nice to me is definitely a new thing. So I tried very hard to remember everything he said so I could write about it to you later.

"Thank you," I said. I wanted to seem polite. Interesting, even. "I like my secret weapon. Although I guess it's not going to stay secret for much longer."

I don't even know what made me say those things. I usually don't talk to other kids at school, ever. Alex just seemed so nice and my thoughts kind of came tumbling out of my mouth before I could think about it too much.

Alex grinned at me. "Your knuckle may not always be secret, but it's still pretty awesome. I don't know what my secret weapon is yet. I'm pretty good at blocking the plate, but I don't know if that really counts. You got any ideas?"

"You made Kyle go away," I reminded him.

He laughed. "Yeah, I guess that could be it. Man, does that guy ever just shut up?"

And then we talked a little more about baseball and the team and stuff. He did an impression of Coach K that almost made me choke on my apple slices.

I definitely did not expect that when the lunch period started!

It's funny, but I'm almost glad Kyle and his friends decided that today was a good day to be mean. Of course, I'd never tell them that!

You've said in your interviews that a good catcher is a knuckleballer's best friend. I don't know if Alex can be my best friend, but does this mean he IS a friend, and not just a boy who happens to be on my team? I sure hope so. It's hard to tell sometimes. VJ, are you really friends with your catcher? Or is that just a thing when you're on the mound?

I think Alex could maybe be my friend. But I don't know for sure.

From,
Vivy

P.S. One week to my first game! Can you believe it?!

Dear VJ,

I know I haven't written in a while, but that's because I'm just so excited about everything and I don't always have time to write. But I haven't forgotten about you, and my first game is in two days. TWO DAYS!

It's not even a sure thing that I'm going to pitch in the game. Kyle the Terrible is the starting pitcher, but Coach K said I should be prepared to come out of the bullpen. So if Kyle messes up, I'm going to pitch.

And even if I don't, I still have to play left field for a while because of the mandatory play rule that says everyone needs to play at least one inning. I really hope I don't drop the ball or something stupid like that. Oh gosh, what a horrible thought! Do you ever worry about these things?

HOW is it even possible to be so terrified and so excited at the exact same time?

Wish me luck,
Vivy

P.S. Alex and I sat together at lunch again. I think maybe he's my friend.

Dear Vivian Jane,

Hello. I'm so glad that I can finally write back to you.

I very much hope this letter arrives in time for your first game. However, I realize that's highly unlikely given the distance between Arizona and Northern California, not to mention the current sorry state of the postal service.

If by chance this letter does arrive before your game, good luck! If not, I certainly hope that it went well for you. I'm anxious to hear all about it. I'd also like to wish you a happy Purim. Your Phil Niekro costume sounds truly inspired—and very appropriate!

Now: On to the main business of this letter.

First, I'd like to apologize for not writing back to you sooner. I receive a great deal of mail and not all of it is very nice. Our team's clubhouse attendant Jacques reads it for me and he recently forwarded some of it to our spring training camp here in Arizona. Your letters were among the most interesting ones and I wanted to respond personally.

As a knuckleball pitcher, I am duty-bound to help the next generation of knuckleballers in any way I can. And when a pitcher is so dedicated to our sport, I feel even more obligated to write back.

I remember meeting a young girl three years ago in the minor leagues and showing her my grip. I'm thrilled to hear you've been working on it for all these years. While some people think the knuckleball is just a cheap trick, not everyone can throw it, let alone command the pitch with any degree of accuracy. The knuckleball is a very powerful weapon when it works and I'm always glad to hear that young pitchers are dedicating themselves to the art.

As you may know, I came to the pitch later in life. When I was in the lower minor leagues, I injured my shoulder very badly—a labrum tear that built up over years. After that, I never could throw a fastball above eighty or so miles per hour. That's not going to fool Mike Trout! After that I took up the knuckleball so I could have a chance at a real career. Now I can't imagine pitching without it.

In response to your question about names, I'm not entirely certain how the knuckleball came to be called a knuckleball. It probably has something to do with the fact that the grip involves clenching your knuckles so tightly. But in any case, you must admit that the word "knuckleball" sounds much more poetic than "fingertipball." I guess the name of the pitch is like so many other things in baseball: It's traditional, maybe a little bit silly, but ultimately very satisfying.

About your being a knuckleballer and a girl: It is my professional opinion that a woman who throws a great knuckleball can compete in professional baseball, like Eri Yoshida. I wish you the best of luck with your pitching and want to hear more about how your season goes. There's nothing quite like your first baseball season, and I do hope you enjoy it—regardless of your final win-loss record. (Of course, wins are always nice!)

I am sorry to hear, if not entirely surprised, that some of the boys on your team are bullying you. People have called me a monkey before, too, and for no reason other than my being a Black man. During one of my college games a whole troop of opposing fans chanted the word at me for three innings before they finally got thrown out of the stadium. (Far too late!) So, yes. People certainly can be awful—not to mention extremely stupid. There's no excuse for such cruelty and I know too well how much it hurts. Even if the people hurling the insults are utter buffoons like Kyle and my own tormentors.

I wish I could say that it ends once you become a grown-up, but that's not entirely true. Even after I reached the major leagues a few years ago and did well, I've had to constantly prove myself to my teammates. It's not always easy being one of a handful of African American guys on a major-league team. Especially when you're also a knuckleball pitcher with a moderately unusual personality. I've heard all sorts of ignorant nonsense over the years: I don't have the starting pitcher mentality, what I do isn't really pitching, the league is going to catch up with me soon enough, et cetera, et cetera. For my part, I say that if throwing a knuckleball were easy, everyone would do it.

This Kyle really does sound like a terrible character, but I hope you won't let him ruin the enjoyment of your season. But I certainly won't give you any of that nonsense about how you should just ignore bullies, because I am all too aware of how hurtful they can be.

I am sorry that your mom is reluctant to support your pitching, but I am confident you will convince her that you belong on the mound. Any girl dedicated enough to work on the most untamable of pitches for three years clearly has an iron will and a truly impressive work ethic.

Just know this: You have another knuckleball pitcher rooting for you.

Sincerely,
VJ Capello

P.S. Thank you for your concern about me, but I am completely fine after last year's World Series. This year is going to be different. I am going to make sure of it.

Dear VJ,

You wrote back! You actually wrote back! Wow, wow, wow! I almost don't know what to say now that I know you're going to read this. But you said you wanted to hear from me again, so I'll try my best.

Even though I wrote all those letters, I guess I never really expected you'd write back. When Nate handed me the envelope and I saw your name on the return address and MY name on the front I could feel my heart zigzag just like one of your knuckleballs. I swear it. Thank you, thank you!

I showed the letter to Dad and he spat up his Coke. It was pretty funny. "Well, how about that," he said. "You and VJ Capello, pen pals!"

I don't really like the word "pen pals" very much. "Pen pals" sounds like something for little kids, and you are a very important grown-up. But it made me happy to see him happy.

He said I should frame your letter and put it on the wall, but that seems pretty silly to me. Why would I want to keep your letter trapped behind glass? Better to put it on my nightstand, so I can look at it and read it again whenever I want.

Dad says it's totally okay for me to write back, and also he wants you to know that he thinks you're awesome. Wow, I'm actually passing along messages to you now.

I could probably go on about how excited I am right now. But you said my letters were interesting and I'm pretty sure going on about how great it was to get your letter isn't very interesting at all. So I'll tell you everything that's happened since I last wrote to you. Mostly my VERY FIRST GAME.

It was Flying Squirrels vs. Cowboys—a home game for us.

When I got to the field, Coach K nodded at me, but Alex wasn't there yet. No one else said hi. That was okay by me. Nerves fluttered around like knuckleballs in my stomach and I didn't want to be distracted by having to Make Eye Contact and Say Something That Sounds Normal. I sat there on the bench and tried to stay sort of calm. Although

I did flap my fingers against the white piping on my pants, so I guess I wasn't very calm at all.

Alex didn't arrive until right before the game started. He rushed in, panting loudly. Coach K clapped him on the back. "Don't be late again, Carrillo," he said.

He sat next to me while putting on all the catcher gear. Alex's hands shook while he was fastening the shin guards, so I helped him out. I've seen Nate do it so many times.

Nate didn't come to the game. He said he had something he absolutely couldn't get out of, but he wouldn't tell me what. Can you believe him, VJ? I bet your brother would never do that. If you have a brother, which maybe you don't. (Do you? Wow, it's so weird that you're actually going to answer my questions now!)

Even though Nate not coming kind of stunk, I also felt a tiny bit relieved. At least I didn't have to worry about making Nate proud when there were so many other things to worry about.

Mom and Dad were in the stands wearing Flying Squirrel bright blue. That was really nice of them, but also kind of strange. I knew Dad would cheer for me, but I guess I didn't expect Mom to get into it so much.

During warm-ups I reminded myself about the agreement with Mom and Dr. Reeve. I decided I would NOT

NOT NOT let bad emotions take over me today. No matter what.

I worried about Kyle doing something Kyle-ish, but he didn't bother with me at all during pregame warm-ups. I guess he's too much of a coward to call me monkey-girl in front of his dad. Really, I don't understand how Coach K can be so awesome and Kyle so terrible. I guess it's sort of like how my mom is this really friendly, talkative person and I'm just . . . not.

Anyway. The game began before I could think too hard about all of it. Coach K and the Cowboys' manager went out onto the field and shook hands. When Kyle marched out to the mound I remembered I forgot to wish Alex good luck. I'd wanted to.

I admit it: Kyle pitched really, really good in that first inning. The Cowboys might as well have been swinging plastic kiddie bats. They made absolutely no contact on his fastball and he struck out three batters on ten pitches. The one pitch that was called a ball looked awfully close to me. Kyle scowled at the umpire after that call, then struck the batter out swinging on the next pitch. I may not like Kyle much—or at all—but his pitching impressed me for sure.

It's a strange thing, watching the game so close up. I could see the individual blades of grass painted white for the foul line. I could hear the WHOOSH of the ball as it flew out over the plate. It was all pretty amazing. Or it would've been if I could have just watched everything like I normally do. I knew there was a chance I'd be pitching. So this wasn't just any old game, and I knew it. I could feel it in my skittering heartbeat and tingling skin.

But Kyle pitched so well it started to seem like I wouldn't get my chance. In the second and third innings, there was only one hit against him—a weak single that probably should've been caught by the left fielder.

Since our games are only six innings total, I started to think maybe I wouldn't get to pitch. The realization was a big relief but also kind of a disappointment.

Except . . . in the fourth inning Kyle got into trouble. After two walks and a hit, a run scored. The score was now 3–1, Flying Squirrels winning. My chest started to feel fluttery, like I didn't quite know how to breathe right anymore. VJ, I didn't know watching someone else pitch would be so tough. Especially since I don't even like Kyle!

Coach K told me to go warm up after Kyle's third walk of the inning. My insides were ready to explode, but somehow I managed to run over to the bullpen area. My first warm-up pitch landed two feet away from the backstop, and the backup-catcher-who-is-not-Alex gave me a big frown. I couldn't even blame him, because that's just embarrassing.

"You're in, Cohen," Coach K told me just a few minutes later.

I definitely didn't feel ready, but it's not like he asked. And Kyle allowed another run while I warmed up. That meant we only led by a single, measly run.

So it was one out, runners on second and third. I got kind of a funny taste in my mouth as I walked up to the mound. Out of the corner of my eye, I saw Kyle stomp back toward the bench. No one looked at him, not even his stupid friends.

Even though I sort of had wanted Kyle to mess up, I couldn't feel very good about it right then. I swear I could feel my breakfast churning around in my stomach. With any luck, it wouldn't end up all over my nice new uniform.

Mom yelled my name—"Vivy!"—from the sidelines. That was nice of her, but I would rather she didn't. I tried to forget about all the noise, the brightness of the sun stinging against my eyeballs. I should be able to pitch through anything. Like you.

Alex grinned at me before I threw my first pitch. "You totally got this, Viv!" he called out.

It was really nice of him to say, but I didn't feel at all sure that I had anything. In that moment I started to regret ever asking Mom and Dr. Reeve to let me pitch. Maybe this whole thing was a mistake. Maybe Kyle was right. Maybe I'm not a real pitcher.

Have you ever felt like this, VJ?

But even though part of me wanted to run far, far away, I forced my feet onto the white rubber. I just had to do what you taught me all those years ago: Throw the knuckleball.

I tried to remember what you look like on TV when you pitch. You're so cool and collected about everything, always. And I wanted to be like you. Problem was, I felt so many different things with so much much-ness. My fingertips felt it too.

The first pitch flew out of my hand and landed way off the plate. I'm not sure how Alex managed to catch it, but he did. The next three pitches weren't much better and I ended up walking that first batter. If a real pitcher did that, the TV announcers would say "that is not a very encouraging start for Vivy" or something. I tried not to think about it.

The second batter came up to the plate. My first pitch was another not-even-close ball. Alex called for a time-out and came over to talk.

"Vivy, you can do this," he said. "You throw that knuckle for strikes in practice all the time!"

"This isn't practice," I pointed out.

"Doesn't matter, you're a knuckleball machine. You can send these guys back to the bench," he insisted.

He gave me a pat on the shoulder and headed back, leaving me all alone out on the mound. I closed my eyes and gulped in about a gallon of air. I didn't know if I really believed anything he said, but his confidence in me made me want to do better, you know? If I failed again, I wouldn't just mess things up for me. I'd be letting Alex down too.

After that I threw two strikes, so maybe Alex's pep talk worked. The batter only managed a weak foul ball that dribbled down the first base line. But my next two pitches were way wide. Ball four.

So I walked in the tying run. My first game ever and I blew the lead because I couldn't manage to throw strikes. Heart hammering, I glanced over to the dugout. Kyle screamed something. I don't know what he said, but it couldn't possibly have been any worse than the things I said to myself.

I waited for Coach K to come in and take me out of the game. I knew exactly what he'd say: "You messed up." "You need to give the ball to someone who knows what they're doing." "You're not a real pitcher."

But he didn't. I don't know if that made me happy or not.

I threw to the next batter. He made contact, but it was only a weak ground ball to second base. The boy after that popped out really quick. Somehow, I made it out of there. I still can't quite believe it actually happened.

It would be a lie to say that it felt good. Everything was way too scary for that, plus I didn't really pitch that well. Even a total loser could get two outs on a good day, probably.

Still. I got two outs.

Your friend,
Vivy

P.S. After I finished Coach K brought in a new pitcher, but we won the game in the sixth inning! Alex got the game-winning double. So that's one win for the Flying Squirrels! I didn't ruin everything after all. Between that and you writing back to me, this has basically been the most awesome-est week ever.

P.P.S. I dressed up as Phil Niekro for Purim celebrations at my synagogue, just like I told you. It went great. Most people didn't know who he was, but I was happy to explain it to them. So that was yet another Very Good Thing that happened this week.

P.P.P.S. People calling you a monkey because of your race is awful! Why are people so mean? I don't think I'll ever understand it.

P.P.P.P.S. Writing all these letters to you is using up an awful lot of envelopes and stamps and paper, which is Very Bad for the Environment. And you mentioned that the postal service is slow and stuff, and that is SO true. I mentioned it to my dad and he said maybe we could talk in emails, if you want. My email is vivylovesbaseball@gmail.com. I'm really sorry if it's not okay to suggest this. I just thought maybe things would be easier this way. If I said something wrong then you can just forget about it.

P.P.P.P.P.S. I know this is definitely too many P.S.s. Sorry. It's just that I wanted to know, is it okay if I call you my friend? I figured that since you taught me the grip AND wrote back to my letter AND said you wanted to hear about my game, maybe it would be okay for me to say that you're my friend. But if you don't think that's okay, I won't do it.

Dear Vivian Jane,

There is so much to cover from your recent letters that I'm not sure where to begin. I'll start with something easy. Yes, you may call me your friend.

I should probably tell you that I may not always be able to respond to your letters quickly thanks to my own pitching and travel. But please continue to write! I'm so curious to hear more about your season. Your descriptions of games really take me back to my own Little League days. I had a terrific team, and a very diverse one too. We had Black kids, Latino kids, Asian American kids, white kids, and mixed-race kids like me too. (No girls, alas, though we undoubtedly could have benefited from talented girls like you.) Baseball was so very fun back then. It's still fun, of course. Just, well, more complicated.

It is rather inefficient for us to keep writing paper letters, and you're quite right that there's another option available. Since your dad is okay with it, I'd be happy to exchange emails with you. My personal email address is vjtheknuckleballer@gmail.com. You can email me there, after you let your parents know. Perhaps you might even show them this letter first. (Hello, Vivy's parents!)

Anyway! It sounds to me like you did just fine in your first game. Better than fine, even. Did you know that I walked the first four major-league batters I ever faced, therefore walking in a run all by myself? Talk about feeling like a total failure. But I survived, and so will you. I'm very impressed that you managed to get the next two batters out after the rough start. That shows nerves of steel.

I am sorry that your brother wasn't there for your first game. I do hope he'll be able to attend future games. To answer your question, no, I don't have a brother. (Unless you count my teammates, but I don't.) However, I do have two younger sisters, so I have some idea about how brothers and sisters are. I know we big brothers can be difficult at times, but I'm sure he still cares.

In the meantime, perhaps you can find other people who can talk baseball with you. Alex sounds like a real treasure. A catcher who can handle the knuckleball is worth his weight in gold, and good people are worth far more than that. He seems like a real friend and I strongly recommend keeping him close. If you don't mind my saying so, you sound a little lonely. Alex can help.

I know you're facing difficulties that are somewhat unique. As I am neither a girl nor on the autism spectrum, I can't really say I know what it's like to be an autistic girl on a baseball team. I'm sure it's hard. As a Black, Ivy League–educated knuckleballer, I know a few things about being an outsider even on your own team. Any one of those things would make me different, but all three of them together makes me quite out of place indeed. Constantly feeling the need to prove oneself can be quite a burden. And after last year, I certainly have a lot to prove. To everyone.

So even though our situations aren't identical, I think I understand at least a little. I'm sure it must be incredibly frustrating to have people doubt your abilities because you're an autistic girl. Can you not try to turn that all into an advantage? Sometimes it's the pitches batters don't see coming that are most successful.

Keep pitching,
VJ

Dear VJ,

Hi again! It's so great to be emailing you now instead of having to bother with paper letters!

Thanks for all your great advice about pitching and Nate and everything. You're probably right. It's just frustrating because I went to so many of Nate's games when he was my age. But now that I'm playing, he doesn't have time for it. Which kind of feels like he thinks my games aren't important. That totally stinks! But I'll try to keep what you said in mind.

I showed your last letter to Dad. He said he wanted to talk to you, so I'm giving the keyboard over to him now. (I hope he doesn't say anything too embarrassing!)

. . .

Hello VJ,

This is George Cohen speaking. I wanted to let you know that I am fine with you and my daughter sending emails to each other. I greatly appreciate your taking the time to respond to her letters. Please let me know if there are any problems. I've attached a copy of my business card with all of my contact information.

Thanks, and go Giants!
George

Okay, this is Vivy again. Hi! My dad is pretty cool, isn't he?

There's more that I want to say, but I have practice in less than an hour, so I should get going.

Well, talk to you again soon!

Vivy

VJ,

I thought I could play baseball. I really did. Just like a normal kid—okay, well, maybe not exactly like a normal kid, but at least normal-ish. But I can't. Kyle and his friends made that very, very clear today.

I'll try to explain everything from the beginning.

"You did all right out there last time, Cohen," Coach K told me at the beginning of practice.

All right is right. I let the tying run score, but then I got two outs. That's not completely horrible, but it's also not great. The first girl to pitch in the major leagues can't just be all right! But it's probably totally ridiculous to even think about that right now.

Kyle the Terrible got really red in the face while Coach K talked to me. "But she let a run score!" he said.

Coach K just stared him down. "Uh-huh. A run that

YOU allowed on base. How about you work on your own pitching and stop worrying about other people, got it?"

Kyle mumbled something under his breath and then he went back to his terrible friends. But not before he scowled at me. What a buffoon! (You used the word "buffoon" and I decided I like it. So I'm going to call Kyle a buffoon from now on—just in my letters to you, of course.)

"Yeah, you did pretty good in the first game," Alex said. "But once you REALLY get going that knuckle's totally gonna demolish the rest of the league. They'll be calling the mercy rule every game."

I smiled at him even though I knew what he said was totally an exaggeration. I looked it up and there is actually no such thing as the mercy rule in our league. There is something called the ten-run rule. That means the game is over if one team takes a ten-run lead. But even if Alex wasn't exactly being accurate about the rules, it's just so nice to have someone on my side after Kyle's meanness.

"Uh-huh. We'll see about that," Coach K said. Although I swear he almost smiled.

I stood next to Alex during warm-ups. It felt very . . . I don't know, nice? Safe? It's hard to explain.

After we finished our stretches and curls, Coach K split us up. He told us that one half of the team would run around the park, while everyone else did batting practice with him. Alex and I got assigned to the running group. Ugh!

But the bigger problem was Kyle. Coach K put him in the running group too.

Ignore him, I told myself. Just run.

Except running definitely is not one of my things. Alex isn't much of a runner either. He's got the classic catcher build: short and squat. "Okay. This is torture," he moaned to me ten minutes into our first lap. "C'mon, we're ball-players! We don't ever need to run this far."

"Mmm-hmm," I replied. I couldn't really think of something smart and interesting to say. I needed to use all my concentration just on putting one foot in front of the other without crashing into Alex. Or collapsing onto the ground. That seemed more and more likely the longer I ran.

"Personally, I think catchers should be totally excused from running laps," Alex continued. I guess he didn't mind me not talking much. "No one expects us to run fast anyway. It's practically in the rulebook. 'Catchers will stink at base running, allowing for easy outs.'"

"What about pitchers?" I said through gasps.

"Yeah, okay. I guess you guys can skip out on laps too."

He sounded like he was going to say something after

that, because Alex always has something to say. But for a long, confusing moment, Alex stopped talking. And when he spoke again it came out all snarl-y. "What the ever-loving heck is HE doing here?"

Alex twisted his face and jerked a thumb toward Kyle. Somehow Kyle the Terrible had ended up only a few feet behind us. He must have run slow on purpose, because he's definitely way faster than either of us.

A sick, twisty feeling crept into my gut.

Kyle caught us looking at him. "Hey, monkey-girl," he said. "Hi, shrimpy."

My eyes prickled a little at the mean name, but I breathed in deeply and reminded myself this was just more of Kyle being a buffoon. This time, I had a friend right here. That had to make things better. Right?

Alex actually laughed out loud. Right then, I liked him even more. "Shrimpy and monkey-girl? That's the best you got?" he said.

Now that he put it that way, it WAS kind of pathetic. I mean, Alex is short. But he's still a super-great ballplayer and Kyle making a big deal about Alex's height makes no sense. And if Kyle's insults about Alex don't make sense, then maybe I shouldn't care what he says about me, either. Right?

It seemed like a Very Important thought. But then . . .

I tripped over a tree root. It came out of nowhere. In an instant, dirt-taste filled my mouth. My knees burned and I yelped.

"Vivy! Are you okay?" Alex called.

Words were really, really hard, but I forced them out. "I'm okay."

In that second, it almost would have been true. I pulled myself up off the ground and stared right into Kyle's square chin. I tried to keep my legs steady while he smirked at me.

"So sorry you hurt yourself, Vivy," he said, drawing out the y-sound in my name. "Here. Let me help."

Before I could even think to dodge out of the way, he reached over behind me and grabbed my ponytail. He tugged it. HARD.

He touched my hair! He actually touched me. VJ, I couldn't help it. I screamed out loud.

Everything was bad. I felt Kyle's slimy hand on my hair long after he pulled away. It oozed from the tips of my hair down to the base of my spine.

Everything was wrong. The world became louder, brighter, more unbearable. Somehow, the sun burned hotter, the boys yelled harder. The wound on my knee stung.

Everything broke. I couldn't think. I didn't know what

to do. I just knew that I wanted Kyle to go far, far away from me and stay away forever. But he just stood there, staring at me.

My body sunk into the ground again. Gravel jabbed against my legs and butt. I think I screamed again, but I honestly don't know for sure. At some point, my brain stopped recording everything that happened, leaving funny gaps in what I remember.

Soon the entire team surrounded me. Coach K stood out in front.

He cut through the crowd to reach me. "Hey, Vivy," he said, his voice really gentle. "You okay?"

I couldn't make myself form words out loud just then, which he took to mean no. I don't know what I would've said anyway. In that horrible moment I just wanted to disappear into the grass so everyone would stop looking at me like THAT.

A lot of the time I think the stuff that comes after is the worst part.

"Hey!" Coach K barked at the team. "This ain't a party. Are you ballplayers or not? Get back to work."

I think maybe Alex said something to me before he started running again, but I don't know for sure. Coach K walked me to the bench and I just knew that everyone was still looking at me. Wondering what the crazy girl was doing on a baseball team.

And the worst part is this: I wondered too.

VJ, I wanted so bad to be on the team. But I knew I'd manage to mess everything up, and maybe not even on the mound. This was worse, because I should have been able to stop it. Should have, should have, should have.

Coach K was really nice about everything, but he didn't let me do anything else for the rest of practice.

And Mom . . . I don't even want to think about what she'll do when she finds out. And she probably will because she always does. And then we'll go through another awful conversation and she'll bug me even more than usual and everything's going to be the worst.

Sometimes . . . sometimes I hate being me.

From,
Vivy

Dear Vivy,

I don't know what I can say to help right now. I don't want to just give you a bunch of words about how everything is going to be just fine. Because I can't promise you that—no matter how much I wish I could. (And please believe me when I say I do wish that. Very much.)

I'm sorry, Vivy. And I'm still on your team. (Well, metaphorically speaking.)

Your friend,
VJ

Dear VJ,

I'm not 100% sure how you can be on a metaphorical team. But that actually does help, a little. So thanks.

Bad things have happened since That Practice. Just like I knew they would.

It's stupid, but I had hoped that after what happened I could somehow just go back to normal. Yeah, what happened was bad—really, really bad—but it's over now. Right? Why do other people need to dwell on it? Can't we just all pretend that it never happened? That would be super-great.

Of course, that's not what happened at all. I barely even finished tying up my cleats at tonight's practice when Coach K came up to me. "Vivian!" he said. "We need to talk. Meet me in front of the batting cage, three minutes."

VJ, Coach K hardly ever calls me Vivian! Heck, he doesn't even call me Vivy most of the time. Usually it's "kid" or "hey you." So when he used my full name like that, I knew it was bad. I just didn't know how bad.

I felt absolutely certain that everyone was watching. Kyle even wagged his eyebrows at me while I shuffled to the batting cage. He mouthed "Bye-bye."

After all that I really, really didn't want to go to the batting cage. But I didn't exactly have a choice.

When Coach K spoke to me, it was in his Quiet Voice. I don't like that voice nearly as much as I like his barking-out-orders voice.

"So. I, uh, thought we might talk about what happened the other day," he said. (I remember everything he said, even all the uhs and umms.)

I noticed that when he talked he didn't really look directly at me, despite the fact that normal people are supposed to Make Eye Contact all the time. Does Coach K need social skills classes? Or was this just one of those moments when normal people don't follow all the rules?

"Okay," I said.

"Okay," he repeated. "Great. So. Does that, um, happen to you a lot?"

I knew that answering this question would be tricky. Obviously, Coach K was asking whether I break down crying and screaming a lot. And my honest answer to that would be, well, how do you define a lot? Once a week? A couple of times a month? But I'm not stupid. I knew that wouldn't be a good answer. I couldn't actually say that and stay on the team.

Instead I said, "I tripped on a tree. That doesn't happen very much at all."

The tips of Coach K's lips crinkled, and I think it might have been a sort-of smile. Not a full smile, you understand. More like a one-quarter smile.

"Good to know," he said. "But I guess what I meant is, do you . . . get upset a lot? Like that?"

"No!" I insisted. Technically, that is 100% true. I've only ever had one meltdown because I tripped on a tree and Kyle pulled my ponytail.

"That's good," Coach K said. He rubbed his hands against his sweatpants. "I've been doing some reading online about autism. I saw some stuff about how people on the spectrum have problems with emotional regulation. But normally you seem so calm and I just—I just didn't know what to think after what happened."

I never understand why people go online to read stuff about autism. I mean, all my teachers say not to trust what you read online! Plus, I'm right here if they want to ask questions about things. I think I'm a better source than Wikipedia or whatever. Although I guess I wasn't exactly being very honest with Coach K about the autism stuff right then, so maybe he was right to look at websites.

"I'm sorry about what happened," I said. "Really, really sorry."

"No, no. You have nothing to be sorry about. I guess this is just a learning experience for both of us, huh?"

"Um, yeah. I guess." I managed enough bravery to look up from my shoes.

Coach K twisted his lips again. This one was at least a one-third smile. "Vivian. If you needed something from me at practice, you would be okay asking, right?"

"Sure," I said.

Of course I didn't actually mean it. I can't exactly ask Coach K to make Kyle go away and also can he stop motorcycles from going past the field because the sound they make is totally the worst. It was nice of him to say, but he can't give me everything I want. I know that.

"Okay, great," he said. "So, is there anything that's been bothering you? Was it just the tree that upset you? Or was there something else that made it worse?"

For a really long moment, I didn't answer. I thought about telling him what Kyle did. But no matter what Coach K said, Kyle is still his son, and the best pitcher on our team. Why would Coach believe the weird special needs girl over Kyle?

Besides, how would I know that Kyle wouldn't somehow find out what I said and then punish me and probably Alex too? I can't do that to Alex after how nice he's been to me!

"No. There was nothing wrong," I said. "It was just the stupid tree. But I'll try to stay clear of them from now on."

Coach K actually chuckled at that. "You do that, Vivy. Just remember that you can always talk to me. I want to help, you know. And I can't do that unless I know what's going on."

His face twitched and he gave me a pat on the shoulder before he jogged off to do other coach-y things. It was a really light pat, which is definitely the worst kind, in my opinion. Still, I think this means that things are okay. Maybe?

Ugh! I don't know anything. Even though Coach K was super-nice, now he's not going to think of me as just Vivy Cohen, knuckleball pitcher on the Flying Squirrels. He's going to think of me as that girl who broke down because of a tree.

From now on I absolutely CANNOT have another problem at practice. Period.

If only I really could avoid all trees! But then there would still be Kyle and his friends.

VJ, I just want to play ball and not have to worry about this stuff. I don't want to be the special needs girl. Not when I'm with the team.

Except, the thing is . . . I don't think it's working out very well. After practice I found a note in my duffel bag, tucked under my water bottle. It was written on yellow notebook paper in black Sharpie: GO AWAY, FREAK.

I don't like being called a freak. But I'm sure it's just Kyle again. Well, 99% sure. It's not like I can just look at a note and magically tell who wrote it. I'm not a TV detective. But it doesn't take any special powers to figure out that Kyle is just being his same old self.

When Coach K said he wanted to know about stuff, he probably meant exactly this kind of thing. I could have showed him the note. Maybe I should have.

In my head I went through everything that might happen if I showed Coach K the note. And I just couldn't see it ending well for me. So I curled the paper up into a ball, stuck it in my pocket, and hid it in my sock drawer when I got home. I thought about throwing it away, but I worried maybe Mom would see it in the trash.

Was not showing the note to Coach K a mistake? I have a feeling you'd say yes. But I'm still not going to do it. Sorry.

I need to forget about Kyle and the note and everything else. I need to pitch well. That will make everything better. Won't it?

From,
Vivy

Dear Vivy,

This is going to be another one of those tough letters, isn't it? If I'm being perfectly honest with you, I don't feel fully capable of giving you the advice you deserve. I know you've mentioned seeing a therapist before. Have you tried talking about this with her? I'm sure she knows more about all this than I do.

But since you've trusted me with some pretty deep stuff, I'll do my best to help. Here's how I see it:

1. Coach K seems like a good man. I know you're not entirely comfortable talking about "the autism stuff" (as you put it), but can you perhaps practice talking to him about your needs? Maybe he can't make the motorcycles go away, but he might be able to help in some other way. I know that if I were a coach, I'd want to help all my players succeed. Maybe that would mean helping people who have needs who are a little different than everyone else. It's not

just about you being autistic. It's about being a good coach to every player so they can play their very best.

2. Yes, I absolutely think you should tell Coach K or someone else about Kyle's note. I'd like to humbly suggest your father. He seems like a good person for this sort of thing.

Maybe I should tell your dad myself. I've considered it, certainly. But after a great deal of agonizing, I decided that it's not fair for me to break the trust you have in me by going to your parents. I want to give you a chance to do this for yourself because I know how important that is to you. But I reserve the right to change my mind.

As your friend, it is my responsibility to advise you. And I am advising you to tell someone about Kyle's bullying. STRONGLY advising, in fact. Do with that what you will.

VJ

VJ,

Oh, please please please don't tell my dad on me! If you do that he'll probably tell Mom and if Mom finds out then I'll never ever get to play baseball again. That can't happen. It just can't.

But you said that I should talk to Dad myself, and I guess you're right. And you've never given me bad advice before. So I guess I'm going to try talking to Dad. He just came home from work—ack!

Vivy

I tried, VJ. I really did. But, well, words are hard and I didn't want Dad to worry about me too much and anyway, I want to do things by myself!

Ten minutes after my last email, I decided to look for Dad so we could have a Very Important Conversation. I found him in the living room, hunched over his laptop. "Hi, Viv-kins," he said.

That was his nickname for me when I was little. But now that I'm eleven, I'm much too old for it. Don't you think so?

I glared. "Don't call me Viv-kins," I told him.

"All right, Vivy," he said. "So, what's going on?"

I opened my mouth. I wanted to tell him all about Kyle and the tree and his meanness and how very scared I am. But my tongue froze in place. Words danced around in my head, but none of them felt 100% right. I chewed on my fingernails. It made me feel better and also made it very hard to talk. Dad didn't say anything else while I nibbled away. I knew he was waiting for me to say something.

"Do you know who won the American League Cy Young Award in 1994?" I finally blurted out.

"David Cone, for the Kansas City Royals," Dad replied immediately. Then he frowned. "Did you really come here to ask me that?"

"Well, it is important information," I said.

Of course, I could have easily looked it up online and Dad knew it. I squirmed. At that moment, I kind of regretted letting you talk me into this. I should have just kept quiet. It's easier that way.

"Okay." Dad fidgeted with his glasses. "So, David Cone is the only thing you wanted to talk about?"

I couldn't look at him. I fixed my eyes on the carpet. There was a small dark stain next to the coffee table—probably a soda spill from Nate. Even though I hadn't noticed it when I first came into the room, suddenly I couldn't concentrate on anything else. Why hadn't someone cleaned it up yet? Didn't they know it would leave an ugly mark forever and ever? I frowned and crossed my arms over my chest.

"I wanted to talk about baseball," I admitted. "Playing baseball, I mean. Not watching."

Smiling slightly, Dad leaned forward. "Sure thing, kid.

You know I never was much of a player myself, but I'm always happy to give some wise fatherly advice."

Okay. This was good. Now I just needed to talk about Kyle.

I could've said, "There's this boy on the team who keeps being horrible to me." That's all I had to do.

Instead I said, "Playing is hard."

"It sure is," Dad agreed. "Do you need help with anything in particular?"

Yet another opportunity for me to say something! "A boy pulled my ponytail at practice the other day." Easy.

But that's not what I said either.

"No," I said. "Just . . . it's hard. Playing on a team. That's all."

Dad's smile completely vanished. "You know, if there's something that's worrying you, you can always come to me and your mom, right?"

"Sure," I said. Or squeaked. Even getting out that one word felt so hard, VJ.

In my head, I wondered whether it would be Unforgivably Rude to just run out of the room. Sandra and Dr. Reeve would say yes, but this was my dad! He doesn't always follow all the rules either. Especially when he's with me.

But even though I itched to run away, I forced my feet to stay glued to the floor. Just like when you're in the batter's box, waiting for a fastball to zoom right toward your chest.

Dad didn't throw a fastball, or even an off-speed pitch. But he did close his eyes and let out a loud breath. "I know all this stuff is hard to talk about," he said after a long pause. "But if you ever want to, I'm still here. 'Kay?"

"Okay," I mumbled.

Then I raced up the stairs back to my room. Where I can write emails to you and never have to worry about not finding the right words at the right time.

I'm very sorry I couldn't follow your advice, VJ. It isn't your fault. Please don't tell my parents? Really, I think I can do this by myself. Like a normal kid.

From,
Vivy

Vivy,

It's okay. I thought talking to your dad might help. But it was never my intention to tell you what to do. You need to figure that out for yourself.

I still wish someone else in your life knew about Kyle's bullying. But for now, I won't betray your confidence.

VJ

VJ,

So you don't think I'm a coward for not telling Dad? Or worse? I know I should be able to tell him things. It seems like it should be so easy. I just . . . can't. And I hate it.

Ugh, I don't want to think about that anymore right now. A whole lot of other things have happened since my last email, and it's all thanks to that stupid thing that happened at practice. I wish there was a way to just erase things as if they never happened. Like maybe once in a while everyone gets to pick five minutes for a total do-over. I'm sure I could do better with the Kyle pulling my ponytail thing if I had a second chance.

Too bad real life doesn't have do-overs.

"We need to talk," Mom said over dinner the other night. She was using her Serious Voice, and I gulped. "I heard you had a pretty rough time of it during practice the other day."

Coach K must have told my parents what happened. I knew he would, but I still felt so sick when Mom started talking. I could almost feel the flood of bad emotions from practice coming back to me, so I forced myself to take slow and steady breaths.

Whenever something like this happens, Mom and Dad always find out. I'll probably have to Talk About It with Dr. Reeve the next time I see her—blech!

Still, even that's not as bad as Talking About It with Mom.

"Honey, I know you don't like to talk about this, but we have to. I'm worried that playing is just too much for you. Coach Kevin said you were screaming at the top of your lungs right there in the park. What could have possessed you? Was it the stress?"

A big frown dominated her face. I curled up my fingers into fists and my nails dug into the skin of my palms. VJ, I remember that game last summer when you got smacked in the knee with a line drive. You had to leave in the middle of a shutout. That's what I felt like in that moment.

"Rachel, are you sure you're not reading too much into this one thing?" Dad asked.

A tiny spurt of hope burst through before I could squash it. Maybe with Dad on my side I can fix this. I didn't want to hope too much, but, maybe . . .

"I'm sure Vivy had her reasons for what she did," he continued.

Dad understands things. Maybe this wouldn't be totally awful. Maybe.

I thought right then about telling them the truth—the whole sorry story of how I tripped and Kyle pulled my ponytail. But I didn't. I guess I didn't see the point. Mom would just fly into another rage and call Coach K. Then Kyle would hate me even worse, and I still might not be able to pitch ever again. So I kept quiet. That wasn't hard, because Mom just kept talking. And talking and talking and talking.

"All the stress of being on the team seems it's just getting to be too much. I've had doubts since the very beginning."

My face got very, very hot. I wanted to point out that I did okay in the first game, but Dad cut in right as I started to form the words in my head.

"Other than this one incident she's been fine," he said.

"I suppose so." Mom's lips still turned in the wrong direction.

"I want to pitch!" I said. FINALLY, I got a chance to say something.

Mom's face finally relaxed, but only a little. "I know you do, but I worry. It's a lot to ask, being the only girl on a baseball team. Even if it weren't for your challenges."

My challenges. Of course. It always comes back to that, doesn't it? And I do know I have challenges, but sometimes I feel like Mom doesn't see all the things I CAN do. I'm not the five-year-old kid who couldn't go to the grocery store without screaming. I've learned things. And I want to learn more, if only I'd get the chance. If only she'd let me have the chance.

You know, a few years ago Nate said he wanted to quit baseball. I don't know why, but Mom and Dad talked him out of it. Now Mom actually wants me to quit! That just doesn't seem right. Is it because I'm a girl? Because I have challenges? Or both?

"Maybe we should talk about this later," Dad said. "No need to make any hasty decisions, right?" He gave me a Special Look.

I never have any trouble figuring out what Dad's faces mean. This one said, "I'm on your side."

At the end of dinner, he gave me a pat on the back and whispered in my ear, "We'll fix this."

And he did! I don't know exactly what he said, but it worked. The next morning Mom and Dad told me I can still pitch. But I have to tell them if anything happens in practice again.

"I want to know everything that happens," Mom said. "I mean it, Vivian. I have to know that you're okay."

Yikes. That doesn't sound very good, does it? But at least I have another chance. And I absolutely cannot blow it. Cannot, cannot, cannot!

Still pitching,
Vivy

P.S. The team played again yesterday and it was a loss. I didn't get to pitch, but I did play a few innings in left field and struck out once. That's not exactly impressive, is it? I hope Coach K doesn't think I can't pitch now. Because I know I can. Or at least I'm pretty sure. Really, could I do any worse than Marty, who started the game and gave up five runs in the first inning? I felt pretty sorry for him, but at the same time I felt glad it wasn't me. Is that bad?

P.P.S. Nate's acting weird again. He's hardly ever in the house anymore, and yesterday he LIED and said he was working on homework in his room when I know for a fact that he wasn't there at all. I went over to ask him if we could throw in the backyard and couldn't find him any-where in the house. I asked him about it later and he just said, "Mind your own business, Vivy."

I'm not sure what's going on with him, but I know I don't like it.

Vivy,

I certainly do not believe that you're a coward. Actually, I think you've got serious guts. And you can quote me on that.

Your idea about do-overs is quite enchanting. I've certainly wanted a few do-overs as of late. In my own case, I wouldn't even need a full five minutes. I'd only need five seconds: the time it takes to deliver a single pitch. I just know that if I could do it all again, I could win.

But that dream is, obviously, quite impossible. No matter how much I wish I could take back that one regrettable pitch, I can't.

Still, even if we don't get any do-overs in baseball, there is the next game. There's always the next game. I am so glad that your parents agree that you should be allowed to stay on the team. Now get out there and throw some knuckleballs.

VJ

Dear VJ,

Oh gosh. I didn't realize talking about do-overs and stuff
would make you think about the you-know-what that happened at the World Series last year. I'm so sorry. I didn't
mean to bring up bad feelings and stuff.

I guess I should probably try to change the subject now.
Okay. New subject, starting now.

I've mentioned before that I have social skills group.
Most of the time I don't like it. At all. But I have to go
every single week, no exceptions. Yesterday was one of
those not-fun times. I try to pay attention and participate.
Really, I do! It's just boring.

At the beginning of every session, we go around in a circle and talk about how the week went. This time I thought
about what to say very carefully. Of course I wanted to talk
about baseball and stuff, but Sandra doesn't like it when I
talk too much about baseball.

"My week was good," I said, repeating the speech I came up with on the drive to group. "I had baseball practice and my throwing sessions went well. At school, we're learning about the American Revolution in social studies. It's very interesting."

"That's great, Vivy," Sandra said. "And how about your family? How are they doing?"

I panicked. I hadn't planned on saying anything about my family, so I didn't have the words in my head. "Um, okay? Except my brother is acting super-weird. He isn't around anymore and I don't like it."

Maybe that wasn't exactly the right thing to say, but I am pretty bothered by Nate's weirdness. It was the first thing that popped into my head.

Sandra nodded. "Okay, Vivy. But just so you know, it isn't polite to say that your brother is acting super-weird. That's a little too blunt. Maybe you can just say he's acting unusually."

"Mmm-hmm," I said.

But really, I thought what she said was awfully silly. Nate wasn't THERE to hear me say that he's acting super-weird, and anyway he really IS acting weird! How is it any different to say that he's acting UNUSUALLY? I don't understand Sandra's rules, really I don't.

I also don't understand the "games" she makes us play.

I don't think they even qualify as games at all. Games are supposed to be fun, like baseball or at least Monopoly. But in group our games always mean pretending to do weird things. (I mean, UNUSUAL things.)

Here's what I mean. Yesterday, Sandra told us we needed to act out meeting a new person. The problem was, Sandra didn't tell us where we were meeting the new person. At school? A baseball game? Stan's Diner in downtown Lakeview? Doesn't that matter kind of a lot?

Anyway, she paired me up with Cynthia, who is the only other girl in the group. I don't mind Cynthia, but I don't think we'll ever be friends. She likes horses and knows nothing about baseball. I don't understand why someone would find a big stinky horse more interesting than the best sport in the world.

Here's how our "pretending to meet each other" thing went:

Me: Hello.

Cynthia: Hi, Vivy.

Me: You're not doing this right! We haven't met each other yet in the game. You shouldn't know my name.

Cynthia: But I know you. We met last year.

Me: Right.

Cynthia: So obviously I know your name is Vivy. What do you think about horses?

I couldn't even get mad at Cynthia for not doing it correctly, because the whole thing was silly and I didn't really care about it.

Oh well. At least I have baseball—and Alex. I don't use any of Sandra's rules with him.

Vivy

I have GOT to tell you about the Flying Squirrels' last game, which happened today. It turns out that Coach K does still think I can pitch, even after that horrible thing that happened in practice. Kyle started the game again, but then Coach K brought me in!

I went into the game to start the fifth inning, so there were no runners on base. That was definitely a little easier on my nerves, but not THAT much easier. Since the score was tied 2–2 it was what the TV announcers call a high-pressure situation. My least favorite kind.

More than anything, I didn't want to be the losing pitcher.

Keep calm, Vivy, I told myself. Keep calm.

Too bad my fingers had other ideas. They just kept shaking, and my first pitch didn't do the knuckle thing. It had a ton of rotation—not at all like a good knuckleball should move. Worse, it kind of drilled the batter right in the shoulder. (Well, not kind of. It definitely hit the batter. Gulp. I hope he realizes that it totally wasn't on purpose!) Anyway, that meant a runner on first base to start off the inning. Not good, not good at all.

Then a new batter strolled up to the plate. I managed to throw a strike for the first pitch, but my fingers still weren't knuckle-ing right. The ball rotated a whole bunch of times on its trip to the plate. (Too many times for me to count!) Luckily, the batter didn't swing. I guess he figured I was just going to mess up again.

Alex flashed me a thumbs-up, but I totally didn't deserve it.

That's when I noticed something. The batter—a gigantic boy with dark hair and a wide smirk—didn't even seem like he was trying. He kept looking back to his friends on the bench and making all these faces. I couldn't quite tell what it all meant, but I knew he was NOT locked into the batter's box like Coach K teaches.

At first I thought this boy was just being annoying, like one of those kids at school who always disrupt class when I am trying to learn very important things. But then I remembered how the other team acted when Kyle pitched. And it wasn't anything like this.

I had that horrible thought again. Were they acting like

this because I'm a girl? It made me so mad, VJ, it really did.

So I closed my eyes, took a really deep breath, and forced my fingers into the grip you taught me. I didn't shake at all.

The next pitch knuckled for real—almost no rotation. It zigged through the air and the boy swung straight through. Strike two.

NOW he started paying attention to me. He stared right at me, which made me uncomfortable. But I tried not to think about that too much. It was a pitcher's count and I had a real honest-to-goodness chance to send the annoying boy back to the bench.

I threw another good knuckleball, but it was pretty wide. Now the count was even at 2-2.

I could still get the out. I just didn't trust myself to do it.

Alex jogged up to the mound. "Hey, so how about we throw this dude a fastball for the next one?" he said.

I thought about it. So far I've only thrown knuckleballs during games. Like I said before, I have a not-very-fast-fastball. Could I really get away with throwing it?

"I don't know," I said. "My fastball isn't very good."

"You can 100 percent do it," Alex insisted. "You don't have to be super-fast. It's the speed difference, ya know? The guy will expect the slower pitch, he swings too late, bam. Strikeout."

I didn't feel sure about this at all. But Alex is my catcher, and Coach K always says pitchers need to trust their catchers. Plus, what he said made sense. So I held my breath and threw my fastball.

I could hardly believe it, but everything went just like Alex said. The hitter didn't expect it and swung too late. I grinned. My first-ever strikeout, VJ!

"Dude, you just got struck out by a girl!" another boy said to the batter as he stalked back to the bench. His friend talked really loud—unnecessarily so, if you ask me.

The batter said something in return, but I couldn't hear what. I'd like to think it was something like this: "That girl has good stuff." But maybe that's just my imagination carrying me away.

Then, I got two groundouts. So I finished the inning without allowing a single run, even after the not-good start.

When I got back to the bench a bunch of the boys told me I did a good job. It wasn't just Alex. Wow! This boy Benny even asked me if I'd teach him how to throw the knuckleball. I showed him the grip, but when he tried to throw it on the sideline things didn't go very well and Coach K yelled at him to stop horsing around for goodness' sake.

I'd have liked to go out there for another inning after that, but Coach K said he wanted to save my arm. I think that means my place on the team is safe. For now, anyway.

Even Mom talked about how well I pitched after the game. "You were amazing, honey. I'm so proud of you."

I almost didn't believe she really said that. But she did!

There were still two bad things about the game:

1. Nate wasn't there to see it. He hasn't been to any of my games so far. I really wish he could've seen my strikeout.

2. The next pitcher gave up two runs in the sixth inning, so we lost. The Flying Squirrels now have one win and two losses. Which is really not very good at all.

But there are also two really good things:

1. Coach K says he wants me to START the next game, which is in THREE DAYS. Three days! Oh my goodness, VJ, I feel so many things right now. But I know one thing for sure: I absolutely, positively have to do well. I need to show Coach K he was right to choose me.

2. Nate promises he'll be there! I'm super-glad he's coming. Except this really means I need to do well. For Nate. But I need to not think about that too much.

Your super-excited (and super-nervous) friend,
Vivy

Vivy,

That's wonderful! Your first strikeout is definitely a big deal.

I very much enjoyed reading your pitch-by-pitch account. Thanks to you, I've been thinking more and more about my own early days playing baseball. I had the best teammates back then, including a catcher who was a little like your Alex—very funny, and one heck of a player besides. Our regional team made it quite far into the Little League World Series before being eliminated by a very good Canadian team. But even that didn't feel terribly crushing, all things considered. It felt pretty great just to be there. No one blamed me for our loss.

In my considered opinion, Alex is right. Knuckleballers can succeed by throwing fastballs, even if they're not the fastest fastballs around. The contrast between the knuckle and the fastball trips up even the most skilled batters.

I can't wait to hear more about your first start. As you probably know, I am also starting a game tomorrow. I certainly hope it goes well for both of us.

Rooting for you,
VJ

Dear VJ,

I did it. I started a game for the Flying Squirrels today. The whole thing was so terrifying and I . . . VJ, I just don't know if I can ever do it again.

All this time I've begged Nate to come to my games. But when he finally came, my nerves multiplied by three jillion. It felt even worse than that very first game. Plus, since it was an away game, we had to drive for almost an hour to get there. As I watched the blur of grassy fields fly past us, my hands got sweatier and sweatier. I thought I'd never be able to grip the baseball with all that yucky sweat pooling up on my palms. (Sorry, I know that's kind of gross.)

Nate patted me on the shoulder once we got to the field. "You're going to do great, Viv," he said.

That was awfully nice of him to say, but it sort of made everything worse. Expectations are hard. It's almost easier when everyone expects nothing much from me.

My legs tingled the moment I stepped onto the field. I knew logically that this baseball field couldn't really be any bigger than ours because league regulations say all fields have to be the same size. But it sure FELT bigger, you know? Plus, the stands were packed full of people, their faces blurring together into one big cloud of eyeballs. I guess baseball must be big in this town.

The other team was named the Whammers, which is a pretty silly name if you ask me. I only hoped they weren't going to wham MY pitches.

I started doing my warm-up stretches on the sidelines next to Alex. That's when I noticed something weird.

At all the other games, no one ever seemed to see me. Except for Kyle, who only talks to me so he can be nasty. But now a bunch of boys from the Whammers pointed at me, whispering to each other. My face got red and prickly. In my experiences it's never a good thing when other people stare. I wondered what mean things they were saying about me.

Except maybe they weren't being mean at all. "You're like famous now," Alex told me with a big smile. "The girl who throws a nasty knuckleball. They're all curious about you. So let's give them a show."

Could that be true? They weren't staring at me because I'm weird, but because I can do something really well? That made me proud, but it also stirred up my nerves all over again. Even the other team expected me to be good! Wow! I guess you're probably used to that, but I'm sure not.

"Hey, Cohen," Benny the center fielder called to me. "You going to win this one for us today?"

"Sure," I said, even though I wasn't even a little bit sure.

Then in almost no time at all Coach K was shaking hands with the other coach and the umpire shouted, "PLAY BALL!"

I wanted to puke. But there wasn't anything in there because I couldn't manage to eat more than a few bites of toast at breakfast.

I thought I knew pretty much everything about baseball, but today I learned something new. It's really terrible to start a game for the visiting team, because you have to wait FOREVER to pitch. And since we scored two runs in the first I had to wait even longer than usual. (Obviously it's great we scored runs, but all that waiting gave me lots of time to think about how very scared I felt. I'd rather just go out there and pitch right away.)

The other Very Big Problem: I had to bat in the first inning. I'm just not good at hitting. I haven't gotten a single hit yet this season. And I especially didn't want to bother with trying to hit right then.

When I went up to bat, there was one out. We had runners on first and third. Since it was my first-ever start, it would be really awesome if I could somehow get a hit. So I tried to concentrate extra-hard at the plate.

I fouled off a few balls and took a few more, getting to a 3-2 count. I started feeling pretty good about things. Maybe I could at least get a walk if not an actual hit.

But then I started thinking about how I'd have to pitch soon and that made me so nervous. VJ, how do you concentrate on hitting when there's PITCHING coming up? It's pretty much impossible! The next pitch whizzed past me before I could even start to think about swinging. So I struck out, for about the bajillionth time this season.

Well, it's a good thing that getting hits isn't really part of my job. Even though striking out stunk, I still felt all right heading back to the bench. I slid my left hand into my glove, just to get into a pitching kind of mood.

As soon as my fingers reached the inside of the glove I knew something was wrong. Instead of just sliding my fingers right in like usual, they got all sticky. Very, very sticky.

I pulled my hand out of the glove as fast as I could. There was gross gunk all over the place. I wanted to scrape all the skin off my hand.

With my heart pounding super-hard, I peeked into the glove. Sure enough, there was a gigantic wad of already-been-chewed gum right in the middle of the webbing.

Ewwww. Someone put this disgusting THING in my glove while I'd been at the plate. And I was pretty sure I knew who.

I tried very hard not to think about the fact that this ball of gunk had been in Kyle's mouth. Tried not to scream, not to flap my hands. I couldn't resist tapping my fingers, though, just a little bit.

"What's wrong, Viv?" Alex asked while he tied up his shin guards.

I showed him the glove and he let out a long hiss.

"Don't tell anyone," I begged. I absolutely cannot be the weird special needs girl who got a wad of gum stuck in her glove. Mom would totally freak if she found out and I'd never throw a pitch ever again. "Please. I just need another glove. Do you have an extra?"

"I only have a catcher's glove! That's not gonna work at all."

He was right, but I didn't know what else to do. My time to pitch was coming up any moment. If I couldn't figure this out, I'd have to pitch without a glove. And I don't think even you can do that.

Luckily, Alex is awesome. He convinced Marty to loan me his glove. Marty wasn't pitching today so he didn't need it. The problem was, Marty has bigger hands than me. So it didn't exactly fit right. But at least I wasn't going out there bare-handed. All I had to do was pitch with a too-big glove. I could do that . . . right?

VJ would be totally okay if he had to pitch with another pitcher's glove, I told myself. It wouldn't bother him at all. You just need to be like VJ.

Except that while I trotted up to the mound I could feel the big empty space in Marty's glove and it was so wrong. I wanted my own glove, which always feels so nice and tight around my hand. Don't think about it, Vivy! I told myself. Forgetaboutit, forgetaboutit, forgetaboutit.

Like I could.

Alex shot me a grin when I got up to the mound. I'm getting more used to his faces, and I thought this one meant "We got this."

I wasn't at all sure we had anything. In addition to the whole glove problem, my warm-up pitches plummeted into the dirt. As though I were still a little kid first learning how to pitch.

The first batter came up. I tried to forget about the glove and Nate and warm-ups and everything.

But I threw a knuckleball that didn't knuckle on pitch number one, and the batter pounded it for a home run. It wasn't one of those barely there home runs either, but the kind of home run that sailed over the outfielders' heads and almost ended up in the parking lot. I could feel what tiny bit of confidence I had slip away.

I managed to get the next boy out on a pop-up. That let me relax a tiny, tiny bit. But then I completely lost the feel of my grip. The next batter hit a bad pitch with a loud CRACK of the metal bat—a double. My knuckle just wasn't knuckle-ing.

At that point I wanted to run away. Go back to the bench, back to my bedroom. Anywhere that wasn't the pitcher's mound.

But I had to face another batter. Amazingly, he managed only a slow grounder to third base. But that soon turned into a Very Big Problem. The third baseman made a wild throw that ended up closer to the stands than to first base. So the runner scored easily, while the batter advanced to second. Our lead was completely gone AND I'd only gotten one out.

I ground my teeth together and tried my hardest not to flap my hands. In my head I understood that the third baseman just made a mistake. It really is hard to catch the ball and then throw it to the right place, all before the batter makes it to first base. I knew that. Still, the error really messed things up for me. Now instead of having to get just one more out in the inning I had to get two, and it was all his fault. Obviously, I couldn't count on my infielders for anything.

But what happened next totally was my fault. 100%. I gave up another big double, and then a line drive single. The score: 4–2, Whammers.

That annoying voice in my head, the one that's always whispering, started to scream. I'm not good. I'm not a real pitcher. I'm a loser.

I managed to get the next two batters out, but they must have been two of the worst hitters on the team. So that isn't exactly something to brag about.

After the inning came to an end I collapsed onto the bench.

"Hey," Alex said to me. "It's okay. We're gonna be okay."

For once he didn't say anything goofy.

No matter what he said, it wasn't okay. A lot of the other boys were looking at me in a not-nice way, and I just knew Kyle and his goons would have something to say about it. Of course he would never give up four runs in the first inning right after getting the lead.

During the top of the second inning, we managed to get another run back. It felt like a gift. I couldn't give it up.

Then it was my turn to pitch again. Before I threw my first pitch of the inning, I closed my eyes as tight as I could, trying to block out all the brightness and noise. I would have covered my ears, but I knew that would just make people laugh and call me a freak.

I opened my eyes. I stared into the web of Marty's glove and stretched my fingers into the grip you taught me. And I threw the ball, hoping it wouldn't rotate. It didn't.

That first batter popped up. I held my breath as the ball rose through the air, but the third baseman caught it perfectly.

Then, a ground ball to second. Again, my infielders completed the play, no problem.

I began to think that maybe I could still save the start. Maybe I could still do good for the team, for Nate, for you.

But on the third batter of the inning I gave up a triple. Bad, bad, and bad. That's when Coach K trotted up and took me out of the game. "Okay," he said, giving me a firm pat on the back.

I'm glad he didn't say "good job," because I didn't do a good job at all and there's no use in pretending otherwise. The Flying Squirrels ended up losing 7–5, with me as the losing pitcher. Coach K says we shouldn't care about personal stats, just team performance. But, well, our team didn't do well and I was the losing pitcher. Which is basically like being a loser, right?

"Greeeeeat job," Kyle told me when his dad wasn't looking. He wiggled his eyebrows all funny so I knew for sure he didn't actually mean it. I searched for Alex, but he was busy fussing with his catcher gear. He couldn't come in to save me. Kyle let out a big, ugly laugh.

People think I don't understand when they do this—when they say nice words that are actually mean. But I do understand people being mean, and I don't like it one bit.

Kyle leaned close to me and whispered into my ear. "You know my dad's not gonna let you pitch anymore after that terrible game, right?"

Only he didn't actually say terrible. His word was much worse, a word you're not supposed to use at all.

I gritted my teeth. VJ, I wanted so much to say something, but I couldn't think of anything that wasn't stupid. So I kept quiet. Which probably still made me look stupid.

But you know what was worse than Kyle? The stuff MY VERY OWN FAMILY said to me when I shuffled back to them with my head down after the game.

"Rough luck, honey," Dad said.

"It's a shame," Nate agreed. "You might have gotten out of the first inning okay if not for that third baseman. Totally incompetent."

I didn't—couldn't—smile back at them. They were just trying to make me feel better and I didn't deserve it.

At least they didn't pretend I did a great job. Mom, though . . .

"Good job, honey," she said.

That made me so mad, VJ. I did not do a good job! Why would she say that? Yeah, Mom doesn't understand anything about baseball, but even she should be able to figure out that giving up four runs plus a triple is not even a little bit good. I didn't even make it out of the second inning!

I frowned at her. "That's not true. I totally sucked."

Normally I wouldn't talk to her like that. This wasn't a normal day, though. My first-ever start and I totally blew it. Couldn't Mom see that something terrible just happened?

Then it was her turn to frown. "You did not suck, and even if you did, I expect better of you than to use that word. There's no need to be so negative. It's just a baseball game."

Just a baseball game! VJ, can you believe that?! I didn't bother to respond—I just grunted and headed for the car. As soon as my butt hit the seat, I took a deep breath and tried to forget everything. Of course, I didn't.

Before he started up the car, Dad whipped his head around to look at me. Squiggly lines popped up on his forehead. That meant he was Concerned About Me. "How do you feel about ice cream, hon?" he asked. "I have it on good authority that all the best pitchers eat ice cream after a tough start."

I'm pretty sure that isn't actually true—right, VJ? Still,

after a game that bad I liked the idea of slurping down some nice cold ice cream.

Even though Mom made one of her unhappy faces, Nate cheered and I said yes. So it was off to Downtown Ice Cream Shoppe. (They make the best ice cream in Lakeview, but I absolutely do not understand why they spell their name "shoppe" when everyone knows the correct spelling is "shop." Duh.)

Once we got there I ordered mint chocolate chip, which is obviously the best flavor. Being surrounded by cool air and ice cream smells made me feel better. Maybe life could be good again. Even after I totally blew my first start.

The ice cream man smiled at me as he handed me my ice cream. It just looked so delicious sitting in the cone, I could almost forget about the game. I bounce-walked to the table where Mom was camped out. Her unhappy face still didn't move a single bit.

Then, on my second-to-last step, my foot dropped to the ground the wrong way and I fell flat on my behind. Mint chocolate chip ice cream splattered all over my chest and face. There was almost nothing left inside the cone.

"Oh, Vivy," Mom said. She rushed over to me immediately, of course.

I whimpered. The ice cream was supposed to make everything better. Or at least make things sort of okay.

Now I was wearing it on my beautiful uniform and all I could think about was that I really am a loser. Of course I can't be a good pitcher. I can't even carry an ice cream cone.

All of it was just too much, VJ. I had managed through the gum and pitching with the wrong glove and getting pounded by the hitters. But this . . .

I couldn't keep up a good face anymore.

At least this time I didn't scream. I just cried.

Mom grabbed a bunch of napkins and started wiping me off, like I'm some kind of baby. All the fussing just made me cry harder and I pulled away from her. I could clean myself. But when I tried to wipe my eyes I just got more bits of ice cream stuck on my forehead, in my hair and eyebrows. Tears, snot, and melty ice cream crept all over my face. Sticking to my skin.

"Let's go back to the car," Mom said quietly.

I didn't protest. How could I?

When I got back to the car, I closed my eyes and pretended to nap. The whole time, I kept thinking about my parents and Coach K and the letter I'd have to write you and how disappointed you'd be to hear about my very first start.

But Mom and Dad thought I was sleeping, so they talked. About me.

"I don't see how we can keep living in denial. This base-ball experiment failed," Mom said. "It hurts to see her so upset."

I sucked in a breath through my teeth. Experiment? I know she doesn't like baseball, but how could she say that?

"Life isn't always sunshine and rainbows," Dad replied.

"I know. Goodness, I know that. But didn't you see what just happened? And does Vivy really need all this baseball stress on top of everything else? What if something happened to her during an actual game?"

"It hasn't yet."

"It could and you know it. Baseball is just so . . . I don't know, competitive. Why couldn't she have picked a less intense hobby, or at least something that would let her be around other girls?"

"Baseball is the greatest sport there is." Dad's voice was soft but firm.

"I'm well aware of your opinion on that subject, but can Vivy really handle it? There was that incident at practice, and then today was a disaster. And you expect me to just smile and let her go off to another game where goodness-knows-what will happen? She's disabled. She can't do this."

Half-asleep, all my energy gone, I didn't shoot up from my seat and demand she take it all back. I definitely wanted to, though.

Oh, who am I kidding? Even if I had been fully awake, I couldn't have said all the things I wanted to say. Not really.

Dad mumbled something else, but I don't remember what because I really did drift into sleep after that. My dreams were full of knuckleballs that didn't knuckle.

So that was my very first start. Not exactly a performance worthy of Mo'ne Davis. Ugh ugh ugh. I don't even want to think about it anymore, not now that I'm almost done with this super-long letter.

Now that I'm done with all that, I'd much rather try and talk about something else. Today's Opening Day! I'm going to watch you on TV with Dad and Nate. Good luck! (I know you won't read this letter until after the game is done, but I wanted to say it anyway.) I just know you'll do better than I did.

Vivy

Dear Vivy,

I'm sorry. That start does suck, and it's okay to say it.

As you undoubtedly know by now, my own first start was something less than ideal. That wasn't how I wanted Opening Day, of all days, to go. I really let myself down with that one. The other guys on my team are too polite to say anything, but I know they must be pretty annoyed with me. I'm annoyed with me. Still, there isn't much to do except look forward to the next game, yes?

I'm sorry the ice cream wasn't much help for you this time, but I do recommend it after tough games. After my own poor start, I indulged in some rocky road. (While I respect your fondness for mint chocolate chip ice cream, I prefer something with higher chocolate content.)

While I don't for a moment believe your Coach K will lose faith in you because of one bad game, I can sympathize only too well with your fears. It has been my experience (and that of other knuckleballers) that people don't fully trust the knuckleball. When the knuckle works well everyone loves you, but when it doesn't . . . well, it can be hard.

But I am talking entirely too much about myself. Quite a boring topic! I'd much rather talk about you and try to figure out if there's any way I can help.

You may not know this, but there's a brotherhood of sorts among knuckleball pitchers. (Well, on reflection, maybe *brotherhood* isn't the most inclusive word.) While I was still learning the knuckleball, many of the greats— Phil and Joe Niekro, Charlie Hough, Tim Wakefield, R. A. Dickey—were very generous in providing advice to me. Even now I know I can ask them a pitching question and get a call back before my next start. I'd like to extend a similarly generous spirit toward you, and do my part to keep the knuckleball tradition going.

I can certainly understand the impulse to replay a bad game over and over again in your head. Believe me: There lies a path of eternal misery. Although pitchers can learn from our mistakes, at this point in your season I think it would be more productive to appreciate victories. And you have enjoyed quite a few of those.

Your friend,
VJ

P.S. I must say that Kyle's sabotage of your glove was quite un-sportsmanlike even by his abominable standards. At this point I'm repeating myself, but: Please consider telling Coach K about it. You shouldn't have to put up with such behavior from someone who is supposed to be on your team.

Dear VJ,

You're wrong about rocky road being better than mint chocolate chip. I just wanted to let you know.

Thank you for the pitching advice. It was very helpful. Have you ever thought about being a coach? You would be really good at it.

Sorry your first start didn't go well. Dad and I watched together. If it helps, Dad thought the umpire wasn't consistent in calling some of those outside pitches. I agreed with him—so unfair! Anyway, it's still just the first week of April. I'm sure you'll find your knuckleball soon.

Baseball stuff has been okay. I pitched two innings in relief yesterday and only gave up one run. I know that's not exactly spectacular, but after my horrible start it was nice to prove that I still can get batters out. Plus we won the game, yay! (The Flying Squirrels still have a losing record overall. I'm beginning to think we're just not a very good team, which is okay with me because it means I have a chance to play, right?)

I'll think some more about telling Coach K about Kyle. Because you asked me to. Right now I can't. But maybe later? Once I figure out the right way to say everything? I don't know.

This isn't about pitching, but Coach K noticed something when we were practicing running the bases today. It turns out that when I run, I don't run in a straight line like everyone else does. Instead I sort of go off track in a diagonal-ish line. I didn't even realize I was doing it. That would be really, really not good in an actual game, because it would take me longer to get from one base to another. If I actually got on base, that is. I haven't yet.

Anyway, Coach K taught me how to run straighter. I just need to look ahead and pay more attention to where I put my feet. If I consciously think about it, I can run better. I'm starting to get the hang of it. But to Kyle, my weird running is just something else that's wrong about me.

Once Coach K started working with the infielders on throwing drills, Kyle came over to me with that ugly smirk of his.

"Hello, Vivy," he said. If I didn't know him, I might have thought he was being nice.

I didn't respond. I wanted to yell at him for the whole

gum in my glove thing. But my mouth wouldn't move no matter how much I wanted it to.

"Right," he said. "Sorry, I forgot. You can't talk like a real person. You know, my dad is only letting you stay on the team because he feels sorry for you. So don't think you can actually pitch or whatever."

Then he laughed like a hyena and walked away.

At least he didn't tug my ponytail this time.

I know what he said is probably just Kyle being mean as usual, but . . . Coach K IS his dad. What if Kyle heard Coach say something about me?

I don't think I could stand that if it were true. But then the other day Coach K put me into the game with a lead, so doesn't that mean he trusts me? At least a little?

Vivy

Kyle is a world-class jerk. I'd like to use another word, actually, but your parents probably wouldn't appreciate my exposing you to that kind of language.

I am glad to hear that you want to talk to Coach K "later," although I note that "later" isn't exactly a real timetable. Perhaps "later" can be now?

VJ

VJ,

But if I tell Coach K about Kyle, won't Kyle just get even madder at me for being a tattletale? Plus, Coach K is Kyle's DAD. What if he doesn't believe me? And also, I've noticed that Kyle acts differently around me than when there are grown-ups around. It's all very sneaky.

Thanks for trying to help, though. Now I'm wondering what word you'd like to use to describe Kyle.

Well, anyway, I have to tell you about something that happened yesterday. Dad and I watched the game together—your game! It's so funny. Normally Dad's the calm one in our house, but when the score is close he gets really worked up about everything. Sometimes he'll even say a Very Bad Word right in front of me.

Since I was very busy watching baseball, I don't remember every word 100% perfectly. But here's what I do remember.

In the fourth inning one of our hitters struck out

looking on a close pitch and Dad made a choking sound. "This ump couldn't find the strike zone if you led him there by the neck," he grumbled. "He's completely wrong about half the calls, and he's not even consistently wrong."

"It is completely unfair," I agreed.

"Yep." Dad made a noise that sounded kind of like *humph*. "But bad umps are part of the game. Really, these guys have got to start doing something on offense."

"Yes," I said. "Especially for VJ's starts!"

I don't want to talk about this too much, VJ, because you already know everything that happened at your start. I know, it wasn't your best game. But really, it's mostly the umpire's fault. You shouldn't feel too bad.

Dad tore his eyes away from the screen and stared at me. "You know, there are pitchers on the team who aren't named VJ," he teased. "But I guess we all have our favorite players. Nothing wrong with that."

"VJ isn't just my favorite player. He's my friend," I explained. You did say I could call you my friend.

"Got it. You're one lucky kid. But if you don't mind me being a little nosy . . . what exactly do you and VJ have to talk about in those emails of yours?"

I started fiddling with the end of my ponytail. Dad knows we talk, of course, but he's never asked WHAT we talk about before. That feels kind of private, you know?

"Come on, honey," he said in his asking-nicely voice. "You don't have to tell me all your deepest, darkest secrets. I'm just wondering. You always seem to be reading your email these days."

I thought about it and decided I could tell Dad a few things about our emails. Even though it did feel a little like revealing something I'd rather keep locked up and close. "VJ and I talk about baseball. And my teammates. And, you know, other stuff."

"Other stuff," Dad repeated. "Hmm. Would that other stuff happen to have anything to do with our family by any chance?"

The answer to that was yes, of course. But I didn't know if it was okay to actually admit it.

"Um, maybe?" I offered. That wasn't a lie.

Dad squeezed my shoulder tightly, which is my favorite kind of shoulder squeeze. "Okay, that's my cue to butt out. You don't need to tell me everything. I just wanted to tell you that it is completely okay to talk about this feelings stuff with other people."

"It is?"

"Most definitely. I know it can be difficult to talk about some things with your mom and me. So if you need to talk to VJ, I say talk to VJ." He paused for a moment. "Hey, wait a sec. Are you going to tell VJ about this conversation?"

I grinned at him. "Maybe."

"Huh," he said. "Wild. Well, you should tell VJ I say hello."

So: Dad says hi.

Vivy

Tell your dad I say hello to him too.

Although I appreciate your willingness to blame the umpire for my failure, this really isn't something you should trouble yourself in thinking about. I'm fine.

I understand your reluctance to talk to Coach K about Kyle. But I don't think you should worry about "tattling." Kyle is being a very poor teammate, and it's affecting you on the field. Informing your coach about what's going on is totally fair. Indeed, one might well argue that you are obligated to do so.

That's my advice. You can take it or leave it. Lately you seem to be leaving it.

VJ

VJ,

I don't mean to leave your advice! I think your advice is
very, very important. I do. But sometimes I just can't do
the things you say. Are you mad at me for that? Please
please please don't be mad!

Well, I want to talk about happier things now. I'm going
over to Alex's house this weekend. He said I should come
over so we could practice throwing and hang out. I wonder
what we'll do.

Before now I haven't really hung out with many kids my
age. Well, except for school, obviously. When I was little
my parents made me go on playdates, but I didn't like
the other kids. Alex is different. I mean, he likes baseball
almost as much as I do. Also, it'll be good to throw to a real
catcher. I haven't been able to throw to Nate AT ALL lately
because he's been so busy.

There's definitely something weird going on with him,

VJ. Last night I woke up because I had to go to the bathroom. The glowy lights of my clock said it was 11:54, which is waaaay past my bedtime.

I tiptoed across the hallway and smacked right into Nate. He was dressed up in jeans that weren't ripped and a nice shirt. Even his curly brown hair was patted down all neat, and he almost never bothers with that. Also, he was humming under his breath. If you ask me, that's a really bad way to not get caught by Mom and Dad.

"What are you doing?" I asked him.

"Nothing!" he insisted. But his voice squeaked and I knew it wasn't nothing.

I made a face at him. "It is something! Why won't you tell me?"

Bad feelings started to poke at me. Not a total storm of horribleness like a meltdown, but I definitely felt hot and prickly underneath my skin. I just didn't understand why Nate lied. He never used to do that! He never used to treat me like I'm a waste of time, either.

"Just go back to bed, Vivy. I don't need you right now," he said, running a hand through his hair. It wasn't quite Nate's Angry Voice, but he was getting there.

I could have threatened him. Could have told him I'd call Mom and Dad unless he told me everything. I didn't do that, of course. That would've just made me even more uncool.

I scowled hard at him before slinking into the bathroom, but didn't say anything more. As I closed the door I thought I heard him mumble, "Thanks, Viv."

Well, at least he bothered to thank me for keeping quiet while he totally broke all the rules. But what is going ON with him?

I don't like the new Nate. I want my brother back.

Vivy

P.S. I wish I had more baseball stuff to tell you about, but last night I had to miss the game because we had our Passover Seder at my grandma's house. Passover is Very Important and it was great to see Grandma. The only problem was, I worried the other Flying Squirrels might think I shouldn't be on the team if I can't play in every game.

When I mentioned this to Dad, he smiled a little. "You know, Sandy Koufax didn't start Game 1 of the World Series because it was on Yom Kippur."

I already knew that, of course, but hearing it again made me feel better about the whole thing. Even though I'm not exactly Sandy Koufax.

Dear VJ,

I know you're very busy with baseball and stuff so I don't want to bother you too much, but a lot of things happened today. Bad things.

Remember that note Kyle left for me a while ago? Well, Mom found it. I probably should have thrown it out a long time ago, but I didn't. I guess I felt like I needed to keep it around. As a reminder. I don't know if that makes any sense.

"Vivian Jane!" Mom yelled. I was on the backyard swing set when she called, so she totally interrupted my swinging. Isn't that kind of rude? I think so.

But Mom did not care about my swinging. She waved the note in front of me and cold bumps instantly popped up on my arms.

"How'd you find that?" I asked.

"I happened to be putting away the socks you very thoughtfully left on your dresser," she replied. "But that's not particularly relevant right now. We need to discuss the more important question. What IS this?"

I stared into the cracks of the backyard dirt, hoping that they could somehow give me a way out. They didn't.

"It's just a stupid note," I said finally. "From this kid on the team. But he is totally a jerk. He doesn't matter."

"Obviously he's a jerk. But honey, why did you keep this in your sock drawer?" Mom asked.

I didn't really have an answer to that. To be honest, even I don't entirely know why I kept that awful note around. So I hugged my arms around my chest and didn't speak.

"I need to talk to your coach," she said after several minutes.

"Please don't!"

"Sorry, honey. You don't get a say in this. Not after you hid this from me for goodness knows how long."

With that, she went back into the house. Her long dark hair whipped around her head and I gulped so hard I gave myself a bad case of the hiccups. Even as I'm typing this, I still feel a bubbly itch in my throat.

She's going to tell Coach K, VJ. What can I even do?

Kind of scared,
Vivy

Vivy,

I want to be honest with you. I'm relieved. I know it's uncomfortable for you, but your mom just wants to help. Perhaps this can be a good thing?

VJ

Dear VJ,

Maybe. I don't know. It's just kind of annoying, you know? I don't need my mom to do stuff for me, I do not!

Here's the thing about Mom. She definitely does not kid around. She told Coach K about Kyle's note. I know this because at practice yesterday he gathered us all around before we even started. He talked a lot about how team-work is important and all of that stuff. I didn't really pay attention to every single thing he said, to be 100% honest. I just wanted to pitch, you know?

Then he said, "Great ballplayers are great teammates. So I don't want to hear about any shenanigans on my team. I find out you've been a jerk, you sit out games. Got it?"

While he spoke, he glanced over at Kyle and his friends. I guess that means he knows how they're actually terrible. Or at least he guesses. I don't know how I feel about that.

During practice Kyle gave me exactly six nasty glares. He didn't say anything to me, though, which is definitely an improvement over his usual meanness. I hope it lasts, but I'm not counting on anything. If anyone knows how to get around the rules, he does.

But I don't want to talk about Kyle anymore. Not when there are much better things to talk about.

Today I went over to Alex's house. It's funny how visiting someone at home lets you learn new things about them. Alex's family just moved here from a town called Arcadia, in Southern California. He lives with his mom and three sisters. "I definitely live in girl-land," Alex told me. "But none of my sisters like baseball! They're the weirdest."

The moment I arrived, Alex showed me to the backyard. It's only about half the size of ours. "Okay. The Cohen-Carrillo throwing session starts right now," he announced.

While we stretched, this little white-and-brown mutt started running around us in circles, barking all the way. His howling hurt my ears and I started to feel a little scared. But Alex told me that the dog—Petey—is all bark and no bite, and after a while I started to believe it. That dog kept up his high-pitched WOOFs all through our pitching session, but he didn't hurt me. I did my very best to ignore all the yapping while I pitched.

I threw about thirty pitches before Alex made me stop. "Coach K will totally kill me if I let you throw too many pitches before tomorrow's game," he said. "We need your arm rested and ready to go."

"I'm a knuckleballer! My arm can take it," I replied. It's 100% true.

He just kind of looked at me for a while. "Vivy, you're pretty hardcore and I respect that. But as your catcher, I'm ordering you not to pitch any more today. And everyone knows that what the catcher says goes. It's one of the rules, look it up."

"Okay," I said. I'm pretty sure that's not actually in the rulebook at all, but the fact that he cared so much . . . well, it felt nice. And I liked that he called me hardcore. I don't think anyone's ever called me THAT before.

After that we played one of those MLB video games, the one with José Altuve on the cover. Alex told me Altuve's his favorite player. "Gotta support another short Latino guy," he said. "Even if he is Venezuelan, not Mexican like yours truly."

"Altuve's pretty good," I said.

"Pretty good?" Alex almost-yelled.

"Pretty great," I admitted.

"Uh-huh. So if José Altuve isn't good enough for you, then who IS your favorite player?" he asked.

"VJ Capello." I stopped myself from adding a "duh."

"I shoulda guessed you'd pick the knuckleballer. He's good. But didn't he blow Game 7 last year?"

VJ, when he said that I started seeing black dots dangling at the edges of my eyes. I swear it. Then I drew in a deep breath and tried to remember that Alex is my friend too. Even though he was WRONG WRONG WRONG.

"It was one pitch," I said after a few minutes of searching my brain for something smart to say. "Doesn't José Altuve ever strike out?"

"Well, yeah. Everyone strikes out sometimes."

"So how can you blame VJ for one bad pitch? He was great for the rest of the series."

"That's fair," he said.

Even though Alex said he agreed with me, I still needed to defend you. I pointed out how you won the Cy Young Award two years ago, in your first-ever season, and finished second last year. How you led the league in innings pitched and placed third in earned run average, the most important statistic for a pitcher. While I talked, I kind of expected Alex to cut in and tell me not to be so boring. That's what usually happens when I talk about baseball to other people. But he listened to everything I had to say and every once in a while he nodded.

"Okay, you win," he said. "VJ Capello is 100% hardcore. And you really know a lot about baseball. Wow."

I've gotten used to Alex's voices, and I could sense surprise there. That surprised me, and the hairs on my arms prickled.

"Of course I know a lot about baseball. I play!" I said.

"Well, yeah, but most of the guys on our team don't know any of this stuff. They probably couldn't even say what team José Altuve plays for!"

Doesn't EVERYONE know that Altuve's an Astro? But then I thought about Kyle the Terrible and his goons. They don't seem like the type to read the box scores every morning. Or ever.

"Plus . . . and don't take this the wrong way, Viv, but you're kinda the quiet type. I bet no one else at school knows how smart and cool you really are."

Frowning, I thought about that for a few minutes. People like Kyle have always told me that I'm stupid, that I talk wrong, walk wrong, am wrong. When that happens you don't exactly WANT to talk very much. But Alex thinks I'm smart. And he's pretty smart himself.

"Just because I don't talk much doesn't mean I don't have things I want to say," I said finally.

"Yeah, you prove that for sure." Alex turned to the video game console. "Now I'm going to kick your butt. Just thought I oughta warn you."

He handed me a controller and started up the game.

Nate has the same one, so I've played it before, but Alex wasn't kidding when he said he'd kick my butt. His skills at the game are definitely José Altuve–level. In no time at all the score was 6–1, him.

While Alex continued to beat me on the screen, his older sister Mariana came in and started chatting with me. Most girls don't seem to like talking with me, so that was pretty surprising, but in a mostly good way.

"Ah. You're the girl my brother's been talking about," she said, lips dancing up.

Was this one of those things where there was more to what she said than what she said? My hands felt all sweaty as I gripped the controller.

"He's my catcher," I told her. I thought that should be enough to explain our relationship, but she still gave a funny smile.

"We're friends, genius," Alex cut in. His cheeks reddened, sort of like we just finished running laps for Coach K. I got warm all over when he said we're friends. I didn't quite understand what Mariana actually meant, but friends are great. "Mari, go away. We're doing baseball stuff and you're so not invited."

He placed emphasis on the word BASEBALL. Mariana looked at the TV and snorted. "I don't think so, buddy. You know how I love getting to know all your friends."

Alex glared. "But you never care about my friends!"

Ignoring him, she plopped down next to me and started asking all sorts of questions. It got really distracting to tell her what kind of clothes I like—jeans and T-shirts, if you're wondering—while also trying to bring home a runner from second base with two outs.

Not that it really mattered. By this point Alex led by seven runs.

"I like her," Mariana announced after question number bajillion.

"Um, thanks," I said. What do you say to something like that, really?

All the therapists say that people on the autism spectrum are too blunt. We need to be more careful in what we say. But Mariana was the most normal-est person I've ever met. And here she was, barging in on our video game and deciding whether or not she likes me to my face. Does that make any sense, VJ?

Actually, I'm glad she did. It's better than what some people do—acting nice to your face and then saying nasty things behind your back. Mariana's pretty weird in my opinion, but she says what she thinks.

I like that.

Then Mariana stood up. "Well, Vivy, if you ever decide

to take a break from this loser and want to do girl things, you know where to find me."

"Um, okay," I said.

"Ugh, girls!" Alex said after she left.

"I'm a girl," I pointed out.

"Yeah, but you're a ballplayer."

I smiled.

Vivy

P.S. Your last start was a little rough again, but that totally doesn't matter. You're still one of the best pitchers in the whole entire world.

Vivian Jane,

I appreciate you defending me to Alex, although it's hardly necessary. I only hope I can justify your faith in me with my performance on the field.

Your emails have been a welcome distraction from the fact that I am now 0-3 on the season. I don't think you understand your own gifts sometimes.

I am also glad to hear you're spending time with Alex outside of games and practice. His sister sounds like a real character, but possibly a friend for you as well. I wouldn't get too bothered by her comments about you and Alex. Friends are most excellent.

Now I really must go watch some videos before my next start. The team hasn't been playing great lately, and I need to fix things.

Hoping both of our knuckleballs knuckle,
VJ

VJ,

Well, of course I am going to defend you to Alex! And I think you're going to pitch great this season. I wouldn't be much of a friend if I didn't think that, would I?

I know you say that you're fine and everything, but sometimes in your letters it doesn't SEEM like you're fine. It doesn't seem like you're fine on the mound, either. (Please please please don't get mad at me for saying that! I'm just telling the truth about what I think.) And I wanted to let you know that if you ever want to talk about your not-fine-ness with me, you can. Because that's what friends do. Right?

Vivy

Vivy,

Please don't doubt that we are friends. We certainly are. However, there's really no need for you to concern yourself with my fine-ness. Or lack thereof. Maybe it doesn't always seem as though I'm fine, but I am. Truly.

So, how are things going with you? Any big games coming up?

VJ

FROM: VIVIAN JANE COHEN
DATE: APRIL 23
TO: VJ CAPELLO
SUBJECT: FINE-NESS AND THINGS THAT HAPPENED WITH MOM

VJ,

Okay, you're fine. That's good. I guess you'll let me know if
that changes, because we are friends.

Sandra says it's rude to only talk about yourself, but
since you asked me about me, I'll tell you what's going on
and stuff.

VJ, do you ever wish you could just drop everything else
so you can play baseball? I do. But I can't. Every Monday
and Thursday afternoon I have social skills group, and
today I didn't feel like going because of my achy-ness. (Is
that a real word? It should be.)

I hurt all over from last night's practice. Coach K's base-
running drills are pretty tough on my legs, and then there
was the throwing session and fielding practice.

"Vivy!" Mom called. "It's time for group."

Even though I didn't want to, I dragged myself down
the stairs. "Do I have to go?" I asked.

I know, I know. When Mom said I could play, I promised to go to social skills group every week without complaining. But when I made that promise I didn't realize just how much baseball would make my muscles ache.

Mom let out a Very Big Sigh. "Honey. We've been over this before. Yes, you have to go."

I bet Mo'ne Davis and Eri Yoshida never had to go to social skills group. But I do and it kind of stinks. I searched my brain for a super-smart argument, something that would make Mom see how I feel. But all I could think to say was this: "Why do I have to?"

Another monster-sized Mom sigh. "Vivy, you know why. Because it helps you develop necessary skills. Now you need to find your sneakers."

"What necessary skills?" I asked her. This was probably a bad idea, but I just couldn't help myself.

Mom ran a hand through her hair and chewed on her lip—a sure sign that she was getting annoyed. "Skills like making friends and having nice conversations with people."

"I have friends," I pointed out. While I talked, I stroked the stitching on my favorite baseball, the one I keep in my backpack. "Alex is my friend."

Normally I wouldn't dare say these things to her. But I

felt achy and annoyed and I guess all my thoughts just kind of spilled out before I could stop myself. Besides, all of it was 100% true. I'm not poor Vivy the girl with no friends, not anymore.

Mom placed a hand on her forehead and rubbed it a little. "I know Alex is your friend, and that's great, but group is supposed to help you develop your social skills more so that when you're older and you need to be independent . . ." Mom trailed off, then stopped talking altogether for a long moment. "Honey, you're really not feeling up to this today?"

"I'm so sore from practice," I told her, drawing out the ooooooh sound in "so."

Mom darted her eyes around the room rapidly, like she had no idea where to look. "Well . . . I guess it would be okay to miss group just this once."

This was so surprising that I dropped my baseball. It hit the floor with a loud thud and I jumped. "Really? Thank you, thank you!"

"You do know it's just this one time," Mom said, raising her voice at the word "one."

"I know."

I raced back to my room so fast after that, flapping my hand a little as I went. Wow! Talking to her actually worked.

I never would have guessed that. I kind of wish I could ask her to just let me quit social skills group altogether, but she'd never agree. This is the next-best thing, though.

Well, let's talk about something better than social skills group: baseball! Your start today was pretty good. Not your best game ever but you gave the team a chance to win. It totally wasn't your fault that the team couldn't score a single run. Those hitters should be ashamed of themselves. You seemed a little mad about it too.

It's funny how everything in baseball is so dependent on other people. You can pitch great and lose some days, and then sometimes you're lousy and win anyway because the rest of the team picks you up.

For the past few games I pitched in relief and did pretty good. Coach K says I'm starting again for our next game tomorrow—yikes! I haven't told him, but it's kind of stressful to go back and forth between starting and relieving. Everything feels uncertain. I don't know what to expect when I go to the ballpark and that just makes me even more nervous than I already am. Which is really, really nervous.

Vivy

Vivy,

While I appreciate your kind words, a great pitcher never complains about hitters not hitting. There's a reason why pitchers get assigned wins and losses when the right fielder does not. It's MY job to win games. Would it be nice if the hitters could score a bunch of runs for me every time? Of course! And yes, I do admit to feeling a bit of frustration about that—just a little! I guess you noticed that. However, I take full responsibility for the loss.

But never mind that. Best of luck to you in your game today!

VJ

FROM: VJ CAPELLO
DATE: APRIL 26
TO: VIVIAN JANE COHEN
SUBJECT: HOW ARE YOU?

Vivy, I haven't heard from you in a few days and I'm a little worried. How did your start go? Are you okay? I know you're busy and can't always find time to email an old guy like me, but I'd feel better if I knew you were safe. I hope it's okay for me to write you like this. I just wanted to check in and make sure that everything's all right.

VJ

Now I'm really worried. Please, Vivy, if you're reading this: when you have the opportunity . . . can you let me know how you're doing?

VJ

Dear VJ,

Sorry you were worried about me. I didn't really think you'd notice that I stopped writing for a few days. I didn't mean to scare you. I just couldn't check my email. Technically I'm not even supposed to be on the computer now.

It's all because something happened at my start. Something bad. I'll tell you more later.

Vivy

Everything started off great. It was just the perfect kind of Northern California day: not too hot, not too cold. The sun got in my eyes a little, but I pulled the cap on tight over my head to block it out.

I remembered everything you taught me. I gripped the ball with my fingertips, right underneath the seams. When I released the ball it floated through the air as though I'd pushed it across a table. Just like a good knuckleball should.

For the first four innings the other team got only TWO hits off me. And one of those was a weak pop-up that fell into that annoying empty space right between the second baseman and center fielder. In total, I struck out three batters and got a bunch of ground balls. The infielders handled all of them perfectly. Alex caught every pitch I threw, even the ones that landed in the dirt. He's such an amazing catcher, I bet he'll make the majors someday.

For once Kyle had nothing to say, though he scowled at me when I sat on the bench between innings. Rude! He ought to have been happy that our team was doing so well. The score was 3–0, us.

"Are you ready to go out for the fifth?" Coach K asked me.

"Yes," I told him, with no hesitation.

He nodded and I jumped off the bench. My arm still felt great.

I started thinking . . . maybe I could throw a shutout. Just like Mo'ne Davis. I mean, obviously it wouldn't be nearly as impressive, because it was just a regular game against the Seabirds, who are tied with us for fourth in the division. Out of six teams. But still. I wanted it so much.

I got the first out of the inning on a pop-up, no problem. Then this huge, hulking third baseman came up. He was so ginormous I could hardly believe he's only twelve years old, though I guess he must be if he plays in our division. His arms were as wide as my legs! He could probably fit right in with Nate's high school team.

Even though it was a little scary to face this boy, I'd done it twice before and struck him out once. I knew I could do it again. On my first three pitches I got him to a 1-2 count.

Alex signaled for a fastball, and I nodded. It totally made sense. If I could throw a good one, right on the corner of the strike zone, maybe he'd have trouble catching up with the faster pitch.

It should have worked.

But my pitch swooshed right over the plate, in that extra-scary place where good hitters never miss. And he made contact, of course he did. Not just the light kind of grounder-to-shortstop kind of contact, but hard, an-extra-base-hit-for-sure line drive.

The ball rocketed straight off the bat. Toward me. It happened so fast, VJ. I think Alex screamed at me to duck, but I froze. The big white boulder soared right toward my head, filling up my sight. And I didn't know what to do.

It hit me in the forehead.

After that I don't remember much. There was a lot of noise. Someone screamed, probably Mom. And the world shook—an earthquake that kept going and going long after it should have stopped.

When I woke up, the grainy dirt from the pitcher's mound was scattered all over the place. It got all over my hands, my face, my once perfect uniform. People were all around and I couldn't quite figure out what was going on. I just knew that the ball had hit me. That my game was over now. There wouldn't be a shutout. I know it was probably stupid to worry about that, but losing the shutout hurt almost as much as my throbbing forehead.

Big arms carried me off the field and soft hands stroked me and I could hear someone yell something about calling for an ambulance. It's all very muddled in my memory, and as soon as the sirens started screeching everything got even fuzzier.

The next thing I remember, fluorescent lights attacked my eyes. Mom's face stared right into mine and her curly hair was flying all over the place. "Vivy, are you all right?" she demanded.

I whimpered a little. Not because my head hurt (although it definitely did) but because of the awful lights and all the noise. The emergency room is so loud, VJ, do you know that? I'd never been there before and after this I don't want to go back ever again.

"Doctor, come here!" Mom said in her Very Loud Voice. "She just woke up and she's hurting!"

A minute later a woman with a blond bun and a stethoscope shuffled over. Her skin was almost as white as her doctor coat. After she said hello, she shone a hard bright light into my left eye. The light hit me and I screamed.

"I told you she has autism!" Mom said.

"Ma'am, I'm just trying to check your daughter's condition." The doctor turned to me. "Vivian, can you try to stay calm while I look into your eyes? I want to help you."

I did not not not want those awful lights in my eyes again. I shook my head. No.

Dad drew closer to me. He'd been sitting next to me the whole time. I just didn't notice because he kept so quiet. "I know this is hard. But Vivy, you just faced down a lineup of tough hitters," he said. "Can you be brave again and let the doctor do her exam?"

I could've pointed out that my start hadn't exactly ended well. Anyway, boys swinging metal bats are way less scary than bright lights and noise all over the place. But even in all the confusing-ness I knew that wasn't going to work. So I gulped in as much air as I could stand. I looked at my parents, then back at the doctor.

"Okay," I said.

"Good girl," the doctor said.

She did her exam and I did my very best not to squirm and scream at all the touching. Finally, it was over. My head still felt like . . . well, like I'd been smacked in the fore-head with a line drive.

"It's probably a concussion, like I thought. We can do an MRI just to make sure there isn't internal bleeding or further damage," the doctor said.

"Do it," Mom said.

The thought of another test made me want to throw up. "No!" I told them.

Of course, they ended up doing the scan. I shut my eyes

super-tight for the whole thing. Even then, I could make out a flash of light when the machine *whomp-whomped*.

Some other doctor looked at the scan after it was done, but I didn't see them. It turns out I just had a minor concussion, like the first doctor said. (I was right! I didn't have to get the extra test after all. Why does no one listen to me, ever?)

I think I would have liked to look at the scan of my brain, but I was still pretty out of it and didn't think to ask. I wonder if people can tell that my brain is different from a normal kid's brain, just from looking at it.

I guess it doesn't really matter. They sent me home with a bunch of instructions about sleep and drinking water and all that stuff. But that was three days ago and this is the first time I'm allowed to use the computer. I had to sneak around just to send you that email yesterday. Mom's only letting me use the computer now because I went to my pediatrician today and the doctor said it was okay to look at screens again.

I should have never thrown that pitch.

I should have tried to jump out of the way.

I should have done . . . something. But I didn't.

It's been almost one whole week. I don't even dare to ask if I can pitch again.

Vivy

Dear Vivy,

I felt so relieved to hear from you yesterday, if more than a little worried about your news. I would have written back right away, but as you probably know yesterday was my start day and I was otherwise occupied.

You have my strongest sympathies. I've had the uniquely horrible experience of being attacked by a line drive while on the mound. (Not quite on the head, but my upper chest. So I have some idea of how much that hurts!)

It happened to me in a college game and absolutely terrified me. When something like that happens, getting out of the way fast enough can be almost impossible. You certainly did not do anything wrong. It's to your credit that you are so eager to return to the game so soon.

I must say, however, that I understand your mother's position. Maybe you should take a break—just a short one!—following such a harrowing experience. I'm sure

Coach K will be happy to welcome you back once you're fully recovered.

And do try not to beat yourself up too much over one pitch.

Best wishes from your friend,
VJ

Thanks for the wishes. And for caring about what happens to me. To be honest, it's still kind of unbelievable that you bother writing to me at all.

I haven't thrown a single pitch since it happened. I really, really want to go into the backyard and just throw a few pitches to the cardboard backstop, but I can't. Mom's been hovering close to me ALL THE TIME and it's the most annoying thing ever. A few days ago when I went back to school she walked with me to the main office just so she could make sure every single teacher knew I had a concussion. So they kept saying "Are you OKAY, Vivy?" for the whole day. Ugh!

I swear, I can barely get her to leave me alone long enough to go to the bathroom. Even while I'm writing this email she's staring at me from across the living room. As though the keyboard is going to suddenly attack me, which would be a very weird thing for a keyboard to do.

Just . . . thank you. For being my friend.

Vivy

P.S. I wish I could just not think about that one pitch.
Really I do. But I can't stop thinking about it and I doubt
I ever will.

I know you're eager to get back on the mound and I get it. But after that ordeal a little rest is well deserved. More experienced pitchers than you have taken breaks after that kind of injury, so don't feel too bad about it. You still have plenty of time to play this season and in future seasons. I have no doubt that you'll soon be pitching again and confounding the boys of Northern California.

Hoping for the best,
VJ

VJ,

I hope you're right. I really do. Things with Mom have been same-y, and that means bad. Yesterday Alex came over to check how I'm doing. That was awfully nice of him, but I wanted to actually PLAY with him at PRACTICE. But of course we couldn't. For once, Nate was around, so I suggested that we throw a ball around in the backyard. I would have had two catchers! That's even better than just one catcher, obviously. But Nate said no way because Mom just might murder him in his sleep if she finds out he let me pitch in our very own backyard. He's probably right.

If you stop to think about it, she's being really illogical. I guess she's scared that a line drive will smack into me again. But that can't possibly happen without an actual hitter, DUH.

Speaking of Nate, something just happened with him. Something I didn't expect.

I guess I've been worried that the real reason he doesn't want to spend time with me anymore is because he got tired of it. Tired of ME. Now he's an important varsity baseball player, so why would he have time to play catch with his sister? Right? But it turns out that's not what he thinks at all.

Last night Mom and Dad were both away at some Autism Foundation fund-raiser. Earlier this week Mom asked me if I wanted to go, but I'm still mad at her for not letting me play baseball, plus I really didn't want to sit through some boring dinner. Isn't it strange that Autism Foundation fund-raisers aren't actually meant for autistic kids? Besides, there was a BASEBALL GAME on and it was one of your starts. I definitely didn't want to miss that.

Nate was supposed to be babysitting me. I don't really need a babysitter at all, but Mom told him he needed to watch over me. That's the rule. So when I saw him all dressed up in khaki pants and a fancy shirt with wide cuffs, I got suspicious. He strolled over to the couch and I caught this truly awful smell. It smelled sort of like Mom's perfume, but worse. Waaaay worse. And that's when I really started to think something weird was going on.

I wrinkled my nose at him. "You stink," I informed him. I thought he ought to know.

"Thanks, Vivy," he said. "But I'm not trying to impress YOU."

"Who are you trying to impress, then?" I asked. "And are you going somewhere? Because that's against the rules. You're supposed to be babysitting me."

Nate's face turned bright red. "Forget about it. I'm not trying to impress anyone. I'm just heading out for a few hours to play some baseball. C'mon, you don't really need me. You're old enough to watch the game on your own, right?"

Even though I totally agreed with him on the babysitting thing, my skin prickled. Nate was supposed to be spending time with ME. Instead he was going who-knows-where to do who-knows-what. I wanted us to watch the game together, like in the old days. Does he really hate spending time with me that much?

"You're not doing what Mom said!" I told him.

"Um, yeah. I know. But I'll be back before Mom and Dad get home. Come on, can't you help me bend the rules just this once? I'll make it up to you, I swear. Maybe next weekend we can go to the park and throw together. I'll tell Mom we're just going to the library or something."

He thinks he can bribe me with throwing time at the park? Well, to be honest, he's right. With Nate's help, maybe I have a chance to pitch again. He must've really wanted to get out if he was going to risk getting in trouble with Mom.

"I thought you were worried she'd murder you in your sleep if you played with me!" I reminded him.

Nate's lips twitched a little. "If you can keep quiet, I'll take that risk."

"Okay," I said. "We have a deal."

"Cool. Thanks, Viv," Nate said. He patted down his hair, which is pretty pointless because his curls never stay down for very long.

Right after he said that, the game switched to a commercial break. That meant I could concentrate better on Nate. I looked over his weirdly formal outfit, the yucky stuff he'd sprayed all over himself. And something just didn't make sense to me.

"You're awfully dressed up for baseball," I pointed out. Then a completely outrageous thought occurred to me. "Are you . . . are you going on a date?"

By this point my brother was purple-faced, but he nodded. "Yeah. I'm going on a date. Now will you stop the interrogation and let me go already?"

I giggled. It's not that I'm against Nate dating, but it just felt so weird to me. I love my brother, but the idea of someone wanting to DATE him just seemed really hilarious.

"Who would want to date you?" I said out loud. I didn't want to be mean or anything, but I wondered about it.

"None of your business," Nate told me. His jaw was clenched all funny. I knew what that meant: He Did Not Want to Talk.

I nodded and turned back to the baseball game. The commercial break was almost over and our best hitters were going to be up soon.

Then, a Really Big Thing happened. And I'm not talking about the leadoff double (although that was cool!).

Nate just kind of stood by the doorframe for a reealllly long time. Not moving at all. I kept my eyes on the TV, but I could still FEEL him looking at me.

This definitely qualified as Nate Acting Really Weird.

"Actually . . ." he began to speak, then stopped.

I waited. Sometimes I think it's best to not say anything and this felt like one of those times.

"Can I tell you something important? Something you can't tell Mom and Dad?" he asked finally.

Well, I didn't expect THAT. I pulled my eyes away from the screen. "Yes, yes, yes! I won't tell. I swear it on my lucky baseball."

He smiled a bit. "You don't have to swear on anything. I just wanted to tell you about the . . . person . . . I'm dating."

"Okay," I said. I have to admit, I was pretty curious about it after all this fuss.

There was another long pause before he spoke again. When he did, his voice sounded different. Almost as though he had trouble talking, like I do sometimes. But that never ever ever happens to Nate.

"The person I'm dating," he said. "It's, um, a boy. From my baseball team. So, now you know."

Nate stared down at his shoes while he spoke, then slowly raised his gaze up to meet my face. Since I knew this was a Very Important Moment, I did my best to keep my eye on his nose—long and straight, just like mine.

I thought about what he just told me. It didn't take very long for me to decide that it's totally cool for him to date boys. Really, I have no idea why some people make such a big deal about this stuff.

"That's very nice," I told him, because it seemed like the Polite Thing to Do. "I hope you have fun with your boyfriend."

To my surprise, he walked over and pulled me into a super-tight hug. It felt a little uncomfortable given the whole smelly-perfume situation. Still, he seemed happy and that made me happy too.

"You're the best sister ever, Viv," he told me. He blinked a few times, and I thought maybe he might cry. He didn't. But if he had, that would have been totally okay.

"Thank you," I said. "And remember, we're throwing together this weekend!"

He laughed. "I wouldn't miss it."

When he walked out of the house, he held his head up high and there was a Very Big Smile attached to his face. Isn't that so cool, VJ?

I hope his date went well. I'm not even mad that he couldn't watch the game with me. Nate trusted me enough to tell me something really, really important. So really, I can't complain.

After he left I went back to watching the game. You pitched okay—not your absolute best, but still good-ish.

While I watched you out there, I thought some more about Nate. Hearing him say I'm the best sister made me glow on the inside. But it also made me realize some very big things.

For months I worried that Nate didn't like me anymore. I thought he was leaving me behind because I'm not good enough. Now I know that he's just had his own life to deal with and stuff. I felt kind of silly about the whole thing. It's just like my dad always says: don't assume things without talking to someone about it first.

I've always assumed that when someone acts mean to me it's because I did something wrong. Maybe that's not it at all, though. Sort of like how sometimes you throw your best pitch and the batter still hits a home run. Because sometimes things just happen and you can't control it. No matter how good and smart and talented you are.

Vivy

Dear Vivy,

You are a good sister and I'm proud of you. I hope you and
Nate enjoy your pitching time together—very exciting!

VJ

Dear VJ,

Oh my goodness, I got your gift in the mail today! I can't believe you sent me a get-well card AND a baseball signed by all the other starting pitchers on the team! Just . . . wow. Thank you.

I put the baseball on my desk, so I can look at it all the time. Even while I'm writing this email I can feel it looking at me, sending good luck in my direction. (I know logically that a signed baseball can't REALLY bring luck, but well, it feels lucky to me. I need every bit of luck I can find after that line drive.) I'd like to hold the baseball in my hand and really get a feel for its ridges and stitches, but I don't want to smudge the signatures. So I am being very careful.

Your (mostly) happy friend,
Vivy

P.S. I hope some of the ball's luckiness rubs off on you for your next start.

P.P.S. There is one Very Good Thing: Nate's acting a lot happier now!

Getting the ball signed was no problem. I hope it brings both of us all the luck we need.

VJ

I know I haven't written in a while. I'm sorry. After you got me a get-well present and everything I should be better about that. I guess I've just been feeling kind of down about things and the idea of writing to you about it just made me feel even downer.

Now that I don't have baseball there are WHOLE HOURS with absolutely nothing to do. I've finished my homework and I feel like I should be at practice but of course I can't go. And the really weird thing is, I can barely even remember the things I used to do to fill all that time!

I mean, I liked reading and Nate and I watched this cool TV show about these kids who solve crimes together, but those things just aren't much fun anymore and I know why. They're not baseball.

Now I don't know what to do with all this free time. So I've been spending oodles of time doing my homework and practicing for my bat mitzvah, which means a lot of reading in Hebrew. I practically have all the prayers memorized by now thanks to all the boring-ness. Things are so bad that I actually looked forward to social skills class last week because at least I got to do something.

Nate kept his promise. We threw in the park last weekend. I had so much fun, and Mom had no idea because Nate told her we were going to the library! But when our time was over everything got bad again. Because who knows when I'll get a chance to pitch again?

I probably don't need to explain this to you of all people, but when I pitch I feel . . . I don't know, bigger, maybe? More important. What I do on the mound matters. It really does. Without baseball . . . well, I'm just the weird girl who isn't good at much of anything.

So today I talked to Mom and Dad about going back.

I begged Nate to help me talk with them about it, but he just shook his head. "Sorry, but I'm keeping my butt out of this one," he said. Traitor.

Thanks to Nate's annoying-ness about the whole thing, I was alone in making my case. I decided to bring it up after my appointment with Dr. Reeve. She said to me, "You're doing extremely well in dealing with all of this," so I thought it would be a good chance. Wrong, wrong, wrong!

Maybe I shouldn't have tried to bring it up right there in the car ride home. But Mom and Dad were both there and we were sitting in traffic so it wasn't like there was anything else to do anyway. It just seemed like a good moment.

I took a deep breath and clenched my fist into the knuckleball grip.

"Can I go back to baseball soon?" I asked.

"I absolutely cannot believe you are even asking that question," Mom said.

"Maybe we can wait to talk about this," Dad mumbled.

"What is there to talk about? We tried something and it failed. I'm really sorry, Vivy. I know how much baseball meant for you. But there are plenty of other sports you can try. You've always liked swimming. Maybe that would work better for you, after everything that happened."

"No! I don't want to!" I didn't realize until the words were out of my mouth that I was yelling—bad, bad, bad.

But really, swimming? I like goofing off in the pool, but that doesn't mean I want to race up and down the lanes like some kind of water rat! Swimming is nothing like baseball at all. I have no idea where Mom gets her ideas.

"You could have died," Mom insisted, voice shaky. "The way that ball came right at you . . . Vivy, it was one of the scariest things I've ever been through. What kind of mother would I be if I just let you go back after that?"

"There's only ever been one person who got killed by a baseball," I told her. "That was a hitter, not a pitcher. In

1920, Carl Mays hit Ray Chapman with a pitch and he died later that day. But that was a hundred years ago! There have been a few pigeons who got killed since then, but absolutely no players."

Mom did not care about Carl Mays and Ray Chapman.

"It was less than two weeks ago that YOU got hit with a baseball, right in the middle of your head. The doctors said you could have had brain damage. Permanently."

"But I didn't."

"You could have."

"I didn't!" I repeated.

I couldn't think of anything else to say. Mom just snorted out a huge sigh through her nose—an ugly sound that pinched against my ears.

"Vivy, honey. I know this is disappointing. But you already have so much to deal with. You don't need to add brain damage to everything else. I'm just looking out for your well-being, because that's my number one job."

I wanted to ask her why she cared if I get brain damage. After all, she thinks I'm already brain damaged, doesn't she? How much damage could another line drive do? IF a ball were to hit me again, which it probably wouldn't, because line drives to the head are very, very rare. I looked it up.

Maybe I could have said some of this to her. But at that point I guess I'd run out of things to say.

"You probably don't even remember this," Mom continued. "But I remember when you were just a little girl and we went to the beach in Santa Cruz and we lost you . . ."

I wanted to growl as Mom started going through this old story. Even though I don't even remember it, Mom talks about what happened ALL the time.

Here's what happened: We were on the beach and I wandered away from Mom and Dad and Nate. I don't remember why I decided to do it. I just did. I was five years old. They couldn't find me, so they called the police and stuff. Then they found me hiding out under a bench on the boardwalk. I saw them and jumped up so I could run toward my parents. But I was pretty clumsy back then, so I tripped and tumbled right down. I ended up with big scrapes on my knees and splinters and stuff. It took a really, really long time for them to get all the splinters out of my skin—not fun at all.

But still. I was just a little kid. I don't get why she's so obsessed with this one teeny-tiny thing. Parents are so weird.

". . . when you came back to me, bleeding, I swore to myself that I wouldn't let anything like that happen ever again," Mom said. "How could I possibly live with myself if I let you go back on that mound, throwing to those boys?"

I didn't bother saying anything else after that. There wasn't any point.

Later, when we got home, Dad whispered, "I'll try talking to her," in my ear.

I tried to smile at him. It's nice that he's on my side. But if I know anything about my parents, it's this: Mom always wins.

Vivy

Dear Vivy,

I'm so sorry this is happening.

While I understand your mother's desire to protect you, you're right: It is, statistically, highly unlikely for a baseball to hit a pitcher in the head. As far as sports go, being a pitcher is pretty safe indeed.

I'd like to make a suggestion. You have so many people on your side, Vivy: Alex, Nate, Coach K, even your Dr. Reeve. And me, of course. Maybe one of them can help you convince your mother to let you pitch again? (I'm afraid that I am not the ideal person for this task, seeing as your mother doesn't know me from Cy Young himself. Long dead though he is.)

You have a team of people behind you. Never forget that, Vivy. No matter how hard everything seems right now.

VJ

You think Coach K or someone would stand up for me if I asked? Wow.

I don't know if it will actually work, but I guess I should try. Maybe. I'll think about it.

Vivy

Dear VJ,

I'm still eating lunch with Alex every day. Even though I'm not on the team anymore. That's awfully nice of him, don't you think so?

We haven't been talking that much about the Flying Squirrels. It just . . , it hurts too much. But today he asked, "So, when are you coming back to practice?"

I gulped. Of course that made my apple juice go down all funny, and I very nearly spewed it all over my lunch bag. Blech!

While I dealt with the whole apple juice situation, Alex just stayed quiet and waited. (And believe me—he talks so much normally that you REALLY notice when he's quiet for a long time.)

"I don't know when I'm coming back," I admitted finally. "Maybe never."

My face became really hot, and I couldn't bear to look anywhere even close to Alex's face. He's awesome, but how can he possibly think I'm this super-cool ballplayer and everything after one little line drive put me out of games for WEEKS? It's so embarrassing, VJ, it really is.

"Is it your mom?" he asked.

"Um, kind of? I mean, yes. Yes, it is. How'd you know?"

"When I went over to your house last week she seemed kinda intense," Alex admitted. I frowned, wondering exactly what she'd said. "But c'mon, you can strike out huge batters with just a knuckleball! Your mom isn't that scary in comparison, right?"

"I guess not," I said. Even though I secretly thought that yes, my mom actually is scarier than a big batter with lots of muscles, I can't tell that to Alex. He wouldn't understand.

"We need you back! Marty can't pitch at all and I'm super-tired of catching him. Promise me that you'll at least try to convince her?"

"I promise," I said quickly. Then took another sip of juice.

Now I have officially promised Alex that I'll try to get back on the team. But . . . I don't think I can talk to Mom all by myself.

So I guess I'll go get help, just like you suggested. I'm

going to call Coach K. Even though I hate, hate, hate talking on the phone!

I really hope it works after all this trouble.

Vivy

Did I mention that I really hate talking on the phone? Mostly I don't do it, except to talk with my grandma Beth. Just the thought of calling someone else made me feel a little sick inside. But I wanted to pitch again so badly. So tonight I found Coach K's phone number on the refrigerator and made the call.

My heart skittered with every ring of the phone. Finally, Coach K's voice came out over the receiver. "Kevin Reynolds speaking."

"Coach K?" I squeaked. "This . . . this is Vivy."

"Vivy Cohen?" His voice got higher-pitched when he said my name. "Good to hear from you. How goes it?"

"Um, okay. I guess." I took a deep breath and reminded myself why I called. "I think I'm ready to pitch again. But my mom won't let me."

"Hmm."

He didn't say anything else. I could feel my last bit of

hope drift away—a ground ball that slipped right past the shortstop's glove.

"Can you help me?" I blurted out.

"No promises, kid. But I'll give it a try."

Wow!!!

I don't want to hope for anything. I know if I dare to hope it won't happen, ever. Like the shutout I never finished. Except . . . I can't help hoping anyway.

Vivy

Vivy,

I'm so glad to hear it! I thought Coach K might be able to
help. If I coached the Flying Squirrels, I certainly wouldn't
want to lose such a dedicated, talented pitcher.

Hoping for the best,
VJ

VJ,

Good news: Coach K does still want me on the team! I know because he called my parents and said so.

"We had a phone call from Coach Kevin today," Mom said at dinner tonight.

My fingers started tapping against the table. I didn't say anything at first. I guess I didn't trust myself to come up with the right words. But I could feel a tiny bit of hope flutter up inside.

"He said you called and asked for his help. Is that true, Vivy?"

I gulped. "Yes."

Mom stared at me for a very long time. "You made a phone call. You."

The way she put it wasn't question-like at all. But I mumbled yes anyway. Her eyebrows shot up so high I thought they might just leap off her face and start dancing on the table, all on their own.

"Well, I have to say I'm proud," Mom said. Those hope feelings fluttered up again in my chest, like a good knuckleball on a cold night. "I know making a phone call like that wasn't easy for you. That's made me think a little. Maybe I've been overly hasty in some of my decisions on the whole baseball issue."

"What does that mean?" I blurted out. I knew it wasn't the Polite Thing to Do, but really! How am I supposed to keep calm at a moment like that?

Mom smiled at me. It wasn't the world's biggest smile, but her lips were definitely pointing in the right direction. That was something.

"It means that we are going to talk about this like grown-ups."

She went on about how she wants to talk with me and Dad at 7:30, in the living room. Because I guess that is what grown-ups do.

Nate grinned at me even as he chewed his broccoli. "Great job, Viv."

I smiled back. Of course, I haven't done anything yet. Not really.

But oh my goodness, VJ! I have a chance. I have a real

chance. Now I just need to Talk About This Like a Grown-Up with Mom and Dad.

Now it's 7:22. EEK.

Still needing your good-luck-wishes,
Vivy

VJ,

Well, something happened. It's not exactly the thing I wanted, but I should be happy. I know I should be happy. And I am happy. Sort of.

I'll try to explain everything. When I got to the living room, Mom and Dad were already there waiting on the couch for me. Except for the fact that Dad didn't put his feet up on the coffee table like he normally does, it didn't really SEEM like an Important Talk for Grown-ups.

"Coach K says that the team has been missing you at practice," Mom began.

That made me feel all warm and stuff inside, so I flapped my fingers. Just a little.

I figured that if this was going to be a grown-up talk, I should say something. "I want to go back."

Dad spoke next, which was kind of surprising. "We know, honey. It's just that your mother—both of us, really—want to make sure that you're as safe as possible."

"Baseball is totally safe!" I protested.

Mom frowned at me, and I realized right away that I'd somehow messed up. "That seems to be a point of debate," she said, then sighed super-loudly. "I know you think I'm being cruel, Vivy. But please understand. I just want to protect you."

There was that word again: "protect." Mom sure says it a lot, doesn't she? It always seems to come up whenever I want to do something and she doesn't want me to do it. Like in second grade, when I wanted to move from special education into a regular class, Mom said she wasn't sure because she wanted to "protect" me from bullies. Even though most kids are way meaner to special ed kids anyway.

I didn't say any of that. Still, I couldn't help the scowl that crept up on my face.

Dad turned to her. "So, if you could be assured that Vivy had some kind of protection, you'd be open to her playing baseball?"

Mom made a face I didn't like one bit. "I don't know," she said. "Maybe."

But what Dad said got me to thinking. "There's stuff to protect you in baseball! Like, you know . . ."

That's when I lost my words and it was all I could do to stop from yelling out loud.

"Like what?" Dad prompted.

"Like shin guards and wrist guards and . . . oh, yes! Yes, yes, yes!"

"Vivy, are you okay?" Mom asked.

"Batting helmets!" I shouted. "I can wear a batting helmet. And not just when I bat, but when I pitch too!"

It was the best idea ever. It really was.

Dad smiled. "It makes sense," he said to Mom. "If another line drive comes at her head, the helmet can protect her from the worst of the impact. I should have thought of it myself."

"Unless I am very much mistaken, a batting helmet can't cover Vivy's face," Mom pointed out.

"Well, yeah," Dad admitted.

I wanted to scream. Does Mom want me to pitch wearing a full mask like a catcher or something?! Hello—how am I supposed to see anything with all those bar thingies on my face? I'd probably end up tripping on my way to the mound. That doesn't sound very safe, now does it?

"Maybe. I don't know. I'm just not sure," Mom said.

It was weird to see Mom not-sure. Normally she's the surest person ever.

I just wanted to scream about how TOTALLY UNFAIR she was being. I didn't. But before I could stop myself, I grabbed a great big clump of my hair. It wasn't all tied up in a ponytail like it is when I pitch, so reaching it was really easy. I could tear it out and then maybe—

"Please, Vivy, don't pull!"

As soon as I heard Mom ask I dropped my hand to the side, but I could still feel my body shaking. It's not like I wanted to do something bad, VJ, but she wasn't making sense and I want so much to play and it was just so unfair! I hate, hate, HATE it.

I hugged my arms to my chest, not daring to say another word.

"Well, maybe we could do a trial," Dad suggested a few moments later.

When he said the word "trial," I let myself feel hope again—if only a tiny, tiny sliver of it. But still. It was hope.

"Hmm. I don't know about that. What did you have in mind?" Mom asked him. She still sounded not-sure.

"Vivy goes to practices, but she won't play in games at first," Dad explained. "Not until you—I mean, we—agree that it's safe for her."

To be honest with you, VJ, I did not like the sound of that "trial" idea one bit. I mean, the whole point of practice is to prepare for the games! That is something so basic even Mom should be able to understand it. I would have really liked to give my thoughts on the trial and how it totally wasn't necessary. But I couldn't because words were hard and Mom was too busy talking to Dad about the saf-est batting helmets and blah blah blah. At some point, I just stopped paying attention to all the boring-ness.

"Okay," Mom said after question number four million. "Vivy, you can return to practice. But you must wear the batting helmet on the field at all times, and no games until I say so. Is that clear?"

"Yes," I said. I had to.

I just . . . I just wished I could feel something close to happiness. Something—anything—besides that awful, empty feeling of disappointment.

"I'm glad we came up with a solution," Dad said. "I'll let Coach K know."

And then Mom fussed with her hair and Dad smiled and talked to me about the history of batting helmets, which I guess weren't mandatory in Major League Baseball until 1971. That's just the kind of weird baseball fact I would nor-mally enjoy, but right then I didn't care much. I couldn't.

VJ, I wish I could REALLY get back to baseball. Not just practice, but real games. I know I could do it. I don't under-stand why a batting helmet isn't enough PROTECTION.

Vivy

Dear Vivy,

That's excellent news! I know it's not everything you wanted, but it's certainly a start. I know you don't want to hear this, but concussions really are serious business. Your mother isn't wrong to insist on taking precautions.

You're still so young, Vivy. You still have so much time left to pitch in games—if not this season, then perhaps next season. There's no need to rush into things right away.

VJ

Dear VJ,

You're usually right about things. But I don't think you're right this time. Sorry.

I mean, I haven't played baseball for WEEKS. The season is more than halfway over already. I just really, really want to pitch in games right now. Not next year! Next year is soooo far away. My mom isn't right! How could she be?

Well, anyway. I don't want to fight with you, so I'll stop talking about Mom. Instead I'll tell you about baseball practice.

Mom and Dad called Coach K and he agreed to their no-playing-in-games rule. Which, I have to say, is totally unfair. But I guess it's still better than not playing at all.

Today I went back to practice for the first time in forever. Scary!

"Hey," Alex called when he first saw me. "Our secret weapon is back. Good to see ya, Viv!"

"I'm not pitching in games," I reminded him. I did explain all of it to him at school, but I wanted to make sure he understood.

He waved a hand to the side. "Yeah, yeah. You'll be in games soon enough. Seriously, Viv, this is going to be the greatest!"

Then he did that thing boys sometimes do, where they thump each other on the back. It was nice, even though I didn't expect his touch.

But you know the really surprising part? Alex wasn't the only one glad to have me back. Benny the center fielder told me the team missed my knuckle, and Jerome the first baseman said he's glad to see me back after what happened. "I don't know if I'd have the guts to come back after something like that," he said.

After a while, I just stopped trying to explain the whole not-playing-in-games thing. I wanted to do what you said and just try to enjoy being at practice and stuff. I could do that—right?

Of course, not everyone seemed happy to have me back. Kyle stared at me with such a fierce scowl that I thought maybe he practiced it at home in front of a mirror. Even his awful friends kept their distance from him and his bad mood.

I thought about what you would say to me. And I tried to just forget about him.

When we started fielding drills, I secured my batting helmet. I'd practiced wearing it for two hours straight last night. At first the feel of the hard plastic against my head bugged me, but eventually I got used to it.

"Nice helmet," Kyle sneered.

He did not mean that my helmet was nice, although it is. But after everything I did to return, I was NOT NOT NOT going to let Kyle ruin my first practice back. Besides, I needed to make up for lost practice time. So I ignored him like adults are always saying to do with bullies. Even though I doubt it'll do any good in Kyle's case.

When it was time for my throwing session, I practically danced up to the mound. Once I got there, I forgot about Kyle and Mom and the stupid trial. It was just me, my catcher, and my knuckleball.

My arm must've been out of practice, because the first few pitches plummeted into the dirt before the ball even made it across the plate. I clutched my glove to my chest, trying and trying to calm my nerves.

I closed my eyes and tried to remember what it felt like to throw a knuckle-y knuckleball. Like I did in that game before I got hurt. But for some reason I couldn't quite find that same feeling in my fingers.

Alex started jogging up to the mound, but I told him "No!"

I closed my eyes and thought about how nice and encouraging you've been. How Coach K helped me get back on the team. I could throw the pitch, I told myself. I could.

I lifted my glove above my head like the pitchers do on TV and released the ball. It flew over the plate way low, but Alex caught it. He shot me a thumbs-up and I felt all warm and glowy inside.

VJ, I really missed this. Not just the pitching, but Alex catching me. Being part of the Flying Squirrels.

Even though I'm not REALLY part of the team. Kyle made that very, very clear to me at the end of practice. I was just sitting on the bench retying my cleats, and he plopped down next to me.

"I don't know why everyone is even wasting time on you," he said. "I mean, you're not exactly going to help us win from the bench, right?"

Then Coach K glanced over in our direction and Kyle gave me a big pat on the back like we're buddies or something. The feeling of his hand on me was UGH. Even through my jersey I could feel that it was sweaty and yucky and just wrong.

Kyle disappeared moments later, but I couldn't forget about what he said.

I had fun at practice. I did. But Kyle's right. What's the point?

Vivy

P.S. I know you had another not so good start the other day, but it's okay. I'm sure the next one will be great.

Dear Vivy,

I'd really prefer not to discuss my own pitching with you. I don't want to fight, either. So I will do my best not to say anything that provokes a disagreement between us.

I know that practicing without the chance to play in games isn't ideal. But there most certainly still is a point to it. The point is to play. To improve. To just enjoy the act of pitching. You can do all those things, even if you don't play in games. Honestly, sometimes I wish I could press pause and just go back to playing for fun.

Come to think of it, I'd like to make an offer. Perhaps I can help you improve your skills. Would it be possible for someone—your father, perhaps—to take a video of you pitching? I can take a look and give you a few pointers. What do you think?

VJ

Wow, thank you! That's a great idea. I'm going to Alex's house tomorrow afternoon, so maybe we can do a video then!

This makes me feel so much better about everything. You are very good at that.

I won't talk about your stuff if you don't want me to.

Vivy

Here it is: the video of me pitching. I hope you like it.

When I told Alex that I needed a video to send you, he made a Confused Face. I forget sometimes that not everyone knows we talk. It's just Dad and now Alex. Not even Nate knows.

"VJ Capello? Are you freaking kidding me?!" Alex exclaimed.

"I would not kid about this," I said.

He still seemed doubtful, so I showed him my email—not the actual emails from you, of course, just my in-box with your name in it. I don't get many emails from other people. When Alex saw the phone screen his eyes got super-wide.

"Totally bonkers-bananas! But now I gotta know: What do you and VJ Capello talk about?" he asked.

For some reason the question made my stomach flip-flop a little. Alex is my friend, but I didn't want to tell him EVERYTHING about our emails. "Pitching," I said. "Duh."

I mentioned the thing you said weeks ago about the way he calls games—that he was smart to call for a fastball after the knuckleball. His cheeks turned completely red and his chest puffed out a bit through his chest protector.

Once he knew the video was for you, he said he had to be in it too. He begged his mom to take the video on my phone, so there it is: me pitching, Alex catching. I've watched the replay a bunch of times. It's so weird to watch yourself on screen. I don't know how you can stand having everyone take videos of you all the time.

As you can see, Alex said "Hi, VJ!" at the very end. I told him I'd say hi for him, but I guess he wanted to say it himself.

Oh, and I'm sorry about all of Petey's yipping in the background. He is a very talkative dog, and for some reason he gets even yippier than normal when I pitch.

Well . . . let me know what you think. If I'm completely terrible you can say so. It won't hurt my feelings. No, actually, it will. But if I really am a terrible pitcher it's better to know for sure now. Before I fool myself into thinking that I might be good.

Vivy

Dear Vivy,

I very much enjoyed seeing you and Alex. Now, for my assessment of your pitching:

I've watched the video several times and can say definitively that you are not a terrible pitcher—not even close. Your form looks sound for someone your age and the knuckleball had great movement. However, I do have a few suggestions for improvement:

1. Your release point looked to jump around a little from pitch to pitch. I recommend that you experiment with different angles, find one you like best, and then stick to it. Remember what it feels like to release a pitch from that exact arm angle and try to replicate it every time.

2. When you pitch, aim your hips right at your target. That will help give you the momentum you need to get the knuckleball just right.

So that's my assessment. I hope you find these suggestions to be at least a little bit helpful.

VJ

You watched the video! And you think my form is sound! Wow. I am definitely going to read that email again and again. I checked my email about eighty bajillion times yesterday just waiting for you to respond. I was soooo afraid you were going to tell me that I'm actually terrible and shouldn't waste my time on baseball. Even though I knew you probably wouldn't say that, because you're so nice.

You do really think I'm not terrible, right? You're not just saying that to be nice? Or because I'm a girl, or because I'm autistic?

Sorry to ask. I just wanted to make sure.

Vivy

Vivian Jane,

No, I am not just complimenting your pitching out of a
misguided sense of niceness. While I am glad to hear you
think I'm nice, I also say what I mean. Especially when
it comes to important matters—pitching most certainly
included.

VJ

FROM: VIVIAN JANE COHEN
DATE: MAY 23
TO: VJ CAPELLO
SUBJECT: SORRY!!!!

Dear VJ,

Sorry. I knew it was a stupid question, it's just . . . well, sometimes it's hard for me to know these things for sure.

When I was in special education, they would make us do silly projects all the time, like building a house out of craft sticks. I never understood why we were had to do such pointless things and I never was very good at them. The glue would always get all over my fingers and the craft sticks wouldn't stick together right. My house always ended up a great big sticky mess. But then the teachers would always say "Great job, Vivy!" even if I made something that looked like dog poop.

Even now it sometimes feels like people say I do a great job when I really, really don't. Like Mom after my first start.

Still, I should have known you wouldn't do that to me. I'm sorry. I'm definitely going to work on the things you told me about.

Vivy

Vivy,

It's okay. I realize now that I was a little blunt in my response to you.

I do wish, however, that you'd learn to believe in your own ability.

You don't really need me to be your cheerleader all the time. Heck, with my current lousy season I'm not sure I should be giving anyone else advice on how to tie a cleat. Let alone the complexities of pitching.

VJ

VJ,

Okay, so we're good now. That's good. (Well, obviously.)

I still think your advice is Very Important. Just so you know.

Vivy

Dear VJ,

Mostly things have been going okay at practice. When I first joined the Flying Squirrels, the boys looked at me funny all the time, especially after Kyle pulled my pony-tail and I freaked out. I didn't really notice how much they looked at me until they stopped doing it. Now I'm just part of the team, like Henry, the other catcher, who always chews gum really loudly. Or Neal, the third baseman, who loves to make fart jokes. ("What's invisible and smells like fish? A cat's fart!" Ugh.)

Obviously I wish I could actually play in games like a real pitcher, but most of the boys are pretty nice about it. Alex keeps saying that I'm going to pitch again really soon, and they all seem to believe it. Of course they don't know what my mom is like. I wish Alex could somehow convince HER to let me play

Anyway, wearing the batting helmet in the field hasn't

been a big deal. Except to Kyle. Ever since Coach K lectured all of us about meanness he hasn't actually left another awful note or anything like that. But he does like saying nasty things when he thinks Coach K isn't paying attention.

"Hey, monkey-girl," he said last night. "Uh, you do know you don't have to wear a batting helmet when you're not batting?"

He laughed like he'd said something super-funny. I didn't want to respond, I didn't, but hearing that hideous hyena snort of his . . . well, it just made me mad.

I looked around the field, but no one else was close. The two of us were waiting to pitch for Coach K. He looked plenty busy trying to fix poor Marty's windup.

"The helmet is for protection against concussions," I said. "Duh."

I knew as soon as the "duh" part came out that I'd made a mistake. Kyle just laughed even harder.

"Whatever. The part I don't get is why YOU of all people need protection against brain damage! You can't break something that's already broken."

I couldn't think of anything to say in response to that. Probably because it's kind-of-sort-of true.

It's not like anyone ever told me that I'm brain damaged or anything. But . . . normal kids don't have to go to therapy and social skills group all the time. Normal kids don't have mothers who worry about every little thing they do and whether or not they have enough PROTECTION. Normal kids don't get called monkey-girl.

I'm not a normal kid. I've always known that. And I want to be okay with it, but sometimes I can't help but think that Mom isn't. When I was younger she made me do this diet that was supposed to help my brain. I couldn't have normal pasta, cake, cookies, and a bunch of other yummy stuff. Mom gave up on it when Dad and Nate kept sneaking me regular pizza. So now I don't have to eat weird food, which is good. But if Mom thought I was fine just the way I am, she wouldn't make me eat fake bread. Right?

Kyle is totally a jerk. But I do wonder about these things.

Vivy

Dear Vivian Jane,

You raise a number of questions for which there aren't easy answers. I'd like to help you sort through it, but I don't want to repeat all the usual platitudes about rising above bullies, blah blah blah. That doesn't help.

Instead I'd like to talk about a subject of mutual interest: the knuckleball.

When you really stop and think about it, the knuckleball is a remarkable phenomenon. According to the usual laws of physics, a ball that doesn't rotate shouldn't be possible. It's completely unique among pitches. Even the wickedest curveball follows a clear, predictable trajectory. A knuckleball that's working will zig and zag, confounding the most talented hitters. You never quite know where it's going to end up—much to catchers' frustration. Make no mistake: What we do is extraordinary.

I'm not very inclined toward science. At Cornell I always

preferred classes in literature and philosophy. But physicists have explained the knuckleball to me like this: The baseballs we throw aren't perfectly even spheres. Oh, the company that makes them says that they're all exactly the same, that the mass is perfectly distributed throughout the entire ball. But it isn't. And thanks to some mechanism that I don't quite understand, the unevenness of the ball makes it possible to throw a pitch that doesn't rotate as it should.

In short, the unique shape of the baseball makes the knuckleball possible.

Of course, brains aren't really like baseballs. I imagine that human brains are even more varied in design. There is no assembly line to produce standardized brains, no computer measuring each brain to meet exact measurements. Out of the billions of people on this great planet of ours, no two brains are alike—not even those of identical twins. So how we can say that one brain is better than another? One might as well try to argue that one sunset is objectively the most beautiful out of all the infinite number of sunsets that ever were and ever will be.

I don't know your mother, so I can't say for sure what she thinks about all this. But I doubt very much that she would agree with Kyle. Who, as you say, is a jerk.

VJ

That makes sense. I guess. Wow, I didn't know all of that about knuckleballs! I need to learn more about science for sure.

Vivy

P.S. Mom still won't say anything about games and it totally stinks.

Dear Vivy,

I am glad you found my thoughts on knuckleball physics to be of interest. Most people fail to appreciate these things, sadly.

Sorry that your mom isn't budging. If I may offer some advice: Perhaps it's time to approach your mom in a different way? Talking is hard, but is there a way you can SHOW her how much you want to play? I know you think it's pointless, but there must be something you can do to help her understand.

VJ

Dear VJ,

Show my mom? How would I even do that? I hope you don't mind me saying so, but that is not very helpful advice.

Your advice is usually very, very good. Like all the stuff you said about brains and knuckleballs. That was really cool. But I don't understand what you mean right now.

I am sorry if this is Extremely Rude.

Vivy

Vivy,

I apologize if you think my advice isn't helpful. I really don't know what else to say at this point. I don't want to tell you what to do. Lately it seems like you haven't been particularly inclined to take my advice at all—leaving me in an impossible position.

That's fine. Your decisions are your own. But I think it's a little unfair for you to insist that your way is best and then get mad at me for not telling you exactly what I think you should do.

I encourage you to act on your own judgment. As always.

Best wishes,
VJ

Dear VJ,

I guess you're right. And I do want to do things for myself, because I am not a little kid anymore.

So I finally did something. Or at least I tried to do something. I talked with my dad on the way home from practice last night.

"You know, honey, I'm really proud of how well you're dealing with all of this," Dad said.

"Thank you very much," I told him.

Dad being proud of me felt good to hear—really it did. But I couldn't help but think, well, if you're so proud of me, then why can't I play baseball?

Maybe it wasn't very smart of me, but I said the thing out loud. In those exact words too.

Dad sighed loudly. That is never, ever a good sign.

"Your mom is really the one who makes these decisions," he said. "I'm sorry, kiddo."

"But why?"

I guess once I start asking these kinds of questions, well, I just don't know how to stop. Even though I probably should have.

This time, Dad didn't speak for a long time. And when he finally did answer, I did not like what he had to say one bit.

"I guess I've always just left these decisions to your mom. I'm not the greatest when it comes to certain things, and, well, I figured she'd know better than me how to help you."

Before I could even think to stop it, a growl escaped from my throat. But I didn't say anything else to him for the rest of the ride home.

Because there was absolutely no point.

VJ, what can I even do?

Vivy

P.S. I know you had another tough start yesterday. I'm sorry. I wish we could both play baseball and pitch great.

P.P.S. I talk to you so much about my problems, but you hardly mention your problems at all. That doesn't seem right to me. So I just wanted to tell you that it's okay to talk about your stuff too.

Dear Vivian Jane,

There's a lot to talk about. I'll try to take it point by point:

1. It sounds to me like your dad means well. However, going to him clearly isn't productive in terms of getting what you want. So, I am going to suggest yet again that you talk to your mom about how you feel.

2. I appreciate your concern. But to put it plainly, I do not want to talk about my baseball performance with you now. Not now and, I must say, not in the foreseeable future. I've already done quite enough talking on this subject with my pitching coach, catcher, and half the sportswriters in North America. I do hope you can respect my wishes in this regard.

In a way, Vivy, you're really quite fortunate. You're young. You still have the ability to make mistakes without the entire world watching. Without having to carry a team on your shoulders. I wish I had that luxury.

I certainly hope you're able to pitch in games again this season. But there's always next year. In the meantime, perhaps you could be doing more to get what you want.

VJ

Dear VJ,

I probably should ask Mom about playing in games. If I could ask her, that is, which I probably can't.

But that's not really what I wanted to write you about. I read your last email again and again so many times, and I still can't believe what you said to me. I know things are tough for you right now and all, but I still cannot believe you said I am FORTUNATE. Just to be sure I had it right, I looked up that word in the dictionary. Fortunate means the same thing as LUCKY. I had a line drive hit me in the face, which is one of the most unluckiest things that can happen in baseball. Plus, I can't even play in games now because my mom is so weird! Personally, I don't think that's very lucky at all. Or fortunate, or whatever.

And you keep saying I should just go and talk to her, but have you even been listening to everything I'm saying? I can't!

AND ALSO, why do you keep saying I can just pitch again next year? That's forever! Besides, if my mom won't let me pitch this year, then she probably won't let me do it next year, either. But you agree with her, don't you? You don't think I should pitch. You just think that I am FORTUNATE. Are you even listening to the stuff I'm telling you?

Okay, so you're pitching badly right now. So what? At least you still get to play. I think that's pretty fortunate.

Vivy

P.S. Are we still friends? I thought we were, but I don't think friends should be annoying and not listen and stuff.

Dear Vivian Jane,

You did not care for my use of the word "fortunate." That's entirely understandable, and on further reflection that was a poor word choice on my part.

I am sorry that you feel like I'm not listening to you, or like I'm agreeing with your mother. I have always tried to give you the best advice I can while still respecting your independence.

However, I must point out that you haven't been listening to me particularly well, either. I did tell you, very clearly, that I do not want to talk about my pitching. Not only did you completely ignore my request, but you also insisted on informing me that I am pitching "badly" right now. While that is quite correct, I would really prefer not to hear that from yet another person.

I'd like to think that we're still friends. But it seems our conversations have become quite unproductive. You're certainly not listening to any of my advice, so I'm not sure what else I can do to help you at this point.

So perhaps it's best if we just not write to each other for a while. That might do us both some good.

Sincerely,
Vincent James Capello

Now you're mad at me. And I'm mad at you too, but I still want to talk. To tell you about my day and baseball and my family and . . . just everything.

But I can't. You said we shouldn't write to each other "for a while." How long is "for a while"? Is it a week? A month? Forever? I'd like to know these things for sure. But I can't ask you without writing. Obviously.

I probably won't send this.

DRAFT DELETED

I shouldn't write you. I know. You said not to.

But VJ, I miss you. I don't have anyone else I can talk to about stuff. Dr. Reeve doesn't understand pitching, Nate still isn't around much, Dad still won't help me, and Mom is still Mom. I guess maybe I could talk to Alex, but I don't want him thinking I'm a total mess and a loser. Even though I kind of am.

DRAFT DELETED

FROM: VIVIAN JANE COHEN
DATE: JUNE 2
TO: VJ CAPELLO
SUBJECT: (NONE)

I met with Dr. Reeve today. The first thing she said to me was, "Well, I hear from your mother that you've been having a rough time of it. Let's talk about it."

I did not want to talk with her at all, so I crossed my arms over my chest and didn't speak. That's when she brought out The Emotions Game. You probably don't know The Emotions Game, but it's the worst. It's sort of like Candy Land because you move your plastic game piece around the board. Except after rolling the dice you have to answer a bunch of weird questions before you can advance to the next space. That's not even a game at all in my opinion.

So I tried to get away with talking as little as possible. Like if the question was "What color would you use to describe your mood?" I'd just say yellow (because yellow is yucky), but then I wouldn't explain my answer. After a bunch of questions like that, she looked at me for a really long time and started asking things that weren't part of the game at all. Why was I upset? Did something happen at baseball practice? At school? I just said no, no, and no. She eventually gave up and we played Connect Four instead. I won two out of three games.

Dr. Reeve isn't the only person who's mentioned that I haven't been in such a great mood lately. Alex noticed too.

Today at lunch he went into one of his usual long talking-thingies. Here are some of the things he talked about: his latest video game high scores, how he wants to redesign the catcher's mask to make it more comfortable and also get rich, and whether or not the grapes his mom packed for him tasted grape-y enough. I grunted a few times, but otherwise didn't say much. Alex talks enough for a whole table of people, and right then I was Not in the Mood for saying a single word.

"Okay, that's it," he announced, popping a grape into his mouth. He chews while he talks, which is a little gross and also not good manners, according to Sandra. "What the heck is up with you? All week you've been wandering around like a zombie. And not even one of those almost-human zombies, but like the guy who gets his head cut off in the first five minutes and then wanders around with a bloody neck stump for the rest of the movie."

"I'm fine." My cheeks burned up about a thousand degrees.

"You're totally not."

"I am. Really." I tried to smile, but managed only a weak grunt.

Alex let out a Big Sigh. "Well, if you won't talk to me about what's up with you, then will you at least mention it to your other good friend? You know . . . VJ Capello?"

He said your name with so much awe, VJ, I wish you could have heard it. I bet you would've been happy. Except, well, I kind of went bonkers the moment it came out of his mouth.

"Don't talk to me about VJ!" I said. Yelled would probably be more accurate.

"Ooookay," Alex said. "If that's the way you want to be, fine. Don't talk to me. Don't talk to VJ. Just act all mopey. Whatever."

Neither of us said another word for the rest of lunch.

I really messed things up, didn't I? Just like I did with you.

DRAFT DELETED

I am sorry that I talked about your pitching, and especially that I said you were pitching badly. That was a Very Bad Mistake. Obviously you don't want to talk about it and I should have just listened to you. There are a lot of things I don't want to talk about, and I wouldn't like it if you sent me emails about them.

I was stupid. Really, really stupid.

I don't even know why I'm still writing when you obviously don't want to hear from me anymore. Maybe because when I wrote to you I never felt stupid or worthless or weird. Until I ruined everything.

Ugh, I'm not going to sen

DRAFT DELETED

I decided that I can write to you after all. I just won't click SEND. I wrote a bunch of letters to you without ever expecting a response. Maybe it's better this way. I can just write what I want and not worry about being stupid or annoying or wrong.

I think Mom noticed that I haven't been very happy lately. She keeps asking "What's the matter, honey?" and "Is there anything I can do for you?" and "Do you want to see Dr. Reeve again this week?" Blech!

No matter how many questions she asks, I will not tell her what actually happened. That's not any of her business and besides, it's not like she can really help. She'd probably just tell me what I did wrong—when I already know that! Ugh ugh ugh.

Now you're mad at me, I'm still not playing in real games, and I was awful to Alex when he was just trying to be nice. Well, I can't fix the first two problems, but I wanted to at least try to fix the third. Yesterday at practice I decided to talk with Alex about some Important Things.

"I'm sorry I got mad at you," I told him when we were doing stretches. "Are we still friends? I want to be friends."

"Um, duh," Alex said. "Yeah. Friends don't stop being friends just because of one stupid fight."

To be honest, that was kind of news to me. I haven't had many other friends before. Except for you, which I absolutely do not want to think about. But it was great to hear that Alex is still my friend, for real.

"Great," I said. "That's what I want."

"Me too. Only . . . is everything okay with you and VJ?"

Part of me wanted to scream at him again. But I knew that would be a very, very bad idea. Instead, I just repeated something that Nate says a lot. "It's complicated."

"Got it. Well, if you ever want to talk about it . . ." Alex trailed off.

"I don't think I'll ever want that. But thank you," I said, hoping that I'd managed to be Polite Enough.

"Okay, got it," he said. "Hey, you want to practice pickoffs?"

So that's what we did. Even though it was kind of pointless because when would I ever need to throw a pickoff if I'm not playing in real games? But at least I didn't completely mess things up with him. That's something, isn't it? Ugh! Also, I don't know why I'm asking you questions when there's no way you'll ever respond.

Wait a sec. I think I hear someone coming.

That was Nate. He's actually in the house for the first time in forever and he wanted to throw in the backyard with me. I didn't really feel like pitching, but there's nothing else to do so I said yes.

My knuckle didn't knuckle and I had zero control. Nate gave up on trying to catch me after only 12 pitches and I couldn't blame him because my pitches all went straight into the dirt.

It doesn't matt

DRAFT DELETED

Dear VJ,

I am very, very, very sorry that I said things I shouldn't have. I know it was a mistake. A very big mistake.

Could you forgive me, maybe? My rabbi says that to get forgiveness you have to say you're sorry, but it's not enough just to say it. You have to mean it and you have to do stuff to show that you mean it. To be honest I don't entirely know how to do that, but I'll try to figure it out because I want to be friends again. And I promise that I am very, very sorry I was mean about your pitching and stuff. Really, I am.

Oh never mind.

DRAFT DELETED

I will not keep writing these stupid emails to you that I never send. I will not.

DRAFT DELETED

I should have just left things alone. Mom said I can't play in games and that's that. Stinks to be me, it's over.

But I couldn't just let it be. Not if there was any chance I could really pitch again.

Besides . . . you kept telling me I should talk to her. And even though we're not writing anymore, I thought that maybe if I could just work up the nerve to talk . . . well, anyway. It was a stupid thought.

Tonight, I knocked on the door to my parents' room. I figured that would be much more grown-up than just barging in like I usually do.

Mom let me in. I should have paid more attention to the frown on her face, but I was too busy trying to remember the speech I planned in my head. As soon as she and Dad were looking at me, I started talking.

"Baseball is a very, very safe sport," I said. "According to this study thing from the people at the Youth Sports Health Foundation, it is safer than other sports like soccer, football, and basketball. When we look at the most popular sports, only golf is safer. But golf is also super-boring."

I waved around the papers I'd printed out from the Internet. Everything I said was right there, written by people with the letters "MD" after their names. I thought it was all awfully impressive.

But Mom was not impressed, not even a little bit. "Vivian Jane," she said. "We have been over this before. We came up with a compromise and it seems to be working out. There's no need to push things too far. Maybe next year we can reconsider."

I probably should have just left it at that. Obviously I don't want to wait another whole YEAR to play in a game, but that's better than nothing. I should have just said yes, okay.

Instead I said, "But I want to pitch in games now!"

"I'm afraid that's just not possible," Mom said. "I've been reading up on concussions. The effects can linger. We can't risk you getting hurt again."

Throughout this whole talk, Dad sat on the bed with a book open in his lap. He watched us SO close, but stayed frozen in place. Not saying a single word. For some reason his silence made me even madder than the stuff Mom DID say.

"The doctors said I'm fine! I want to play," I said. That was probably another Very Big Mistake.

"Well, I'm afraid that what you want isn't the most relevant thing right now. I'm concerned about what you need. And I have to say that all this yelling isn't exactly convincing me that you can handle playing baseball!" Mom said. She was getting mad and madder, for sure.

"I did okay at games!" I said—well, screamed. "I did!"

My stack of papers plummeted to the floor quicker than a sinking fastball in the dirt.

"Well, yes, you did okay. Except for the small incident of you getting nearly killed by that ball. Not to mention your problems at practice. And acting snappish after games whenever things didn't go your way. Shall I go on?"

Mom wasn't talking quite as loudly as me, but she was definitely louder than usual. Normally I would have shrunk back at the sound, but at that moment I didn't. All I knew was that I felt too much. Way, way too much.

"You're not being fair!" I yelled.

Or at least that's what I tried to say. A few words into it I just kind of shrieked out something that wasn't a real sentence at all. What I actually said went something like arghhhhhhnonononononononpleasepleasepleasenotfair.

Mom said another shouty thing. Even Dad finally started to talk. But I didn't really take any of it in. My brain screamed at me and it wouldn't shut up. So I attacked my own hair. My fingers trembled so much I couldn't actually grip the strands, but I wanted so much to just tear it all out. Rip off my skin. Do something—anything—that would help me feel something besides the horribleness. Except the horrible had already seeped all over me. It got underneath my fingernails. Between my teeth. Into the spaces between my toes. I couldn't get away from it.

I curled myself up into a tight ball on the floor and tried to pretend I had fallen into some other universe. I am nothing, I told myself. I am nothing and this is not happening to me.

With my face down, I inhaled the disgusting smell of carpet. It made me cough and hiccup and cough again. I was surrounded by tears and snot and all the gross terrible things.

I couldn't escape. Couldn't even budge from my ball.

Soon Mom and Dad both stopped talking. Dad came over and wrapped me up into a tight hug. "Shhh," he whispered into my ear. "Vivy. Vivy, sweetie. It's all right. It's going to be all right."

Before I could stop myself, I started to rock. Instead of telling me not to, he joined me.

As we rocked on the floor together, back and forth, back and forth, I started to think that maybe everything wasn't completely terrible. But it was mostly terrible.

Still. I knew I had to get it together, at least a little bit.

And it wasn't even about playing in games. I figured the chances of THAT happening were zero. But if I couldn't try to calm myself, well, who knows what Mom might do?

After several minutes—or was it several dozen?—my breathing slowed. My mind cleared. Dad lifted me and carried me into my room. I should have been annoyed at being treated like a baby, but I just felt too tired to care.

Dad kissed me on the forehead after he settled me into bed. I pulled the covers over my head and didn't budge from that position until about ten minutes ago, when I dragged myself to the computer and started writing this email. An email that I won't even send. I just . . . I didn't know what else to do. I still don't.

I wish I could talk to you about this for real. Even if it is completely and totally humiliating, I still want to talk to someone who might understand.

Everything's just so impossible now. And unlike that stupid line drive that ruined everything, this is all my fault. 100%.

DRAFT DELETED

I am never ever going to send this, but I am pretending that this is a normal letter. Even though it's not, and nothing has been normal since That Thing.

Mom hasn't punished me, but she has been acting really weird. She asks me if I'm feeling well about ten bajillion times per day and talks to me in this weird-soft voice. Honestly, I wish she'd just say I have to clean out the kitchen cabinets as punishment.

At least not absolutely everything has been completely stinky. Today Nate came up to chat with me while I was on my swing in the backyard. I smiled really wide, to let him know how happy it made me to see him.

"How goes it, Viv?" he asked.

I slowed down the swing so I could concentrate on talking. "Okay," I said.

"Just okay?"

"Baseball. Mom. Things." I didn't need to say anything else.

"Ah. Got it."

Nate sat down on the swing next to mine, even though he doesn't really fit anymore. It was kind of funny—a tall, muscle-y boy sitting in a kid's swing, his legs hanging out all weird. For a few moments, we just sat there in mostly comfy silence. Even though it's slightly pointless to sit on a swing and not actually swing, I felt glad to have time with Nate.

"Have you thought about talking to Mom and Dad?" Nate asked finally.

I did not like hearing that one little bit, so I glared at him. Of course he didn't understand my problem. But I tried to explain anyway.

"Talking to Mom is just so hard!" I said. "And then she doesn't listen and I just do it wrong and everything goes bad."

To be honest, I didn't think he would get it. Not really. Talking to people is never hard for Nate. He's just like Mom that way.

But he surprised me. "I can definitely understand that," he said, staring off into the distance.

"You can?" I thought about it for a little while, and then everything started to make sense. "Oh right. You still haven't told them about . . . you."

I haven't really thought about that for a while.

Everything's been so terrible with you and Mom and base-ball, I haven't been thinking about Nate very much at all. That's wrong. I should have tried to do something for my brother. I don't know what, but I should have at least made my best effort. Coach K says that team players put their best effort into everything. But I guess I'm not giving any-thing my best effort right now.

Nate looked at me. "You can say gay. I'm gay. I just don't know how to tell them, you know?"

"Why not?" I asked.

I realized as soon as I spoke that maybe my question was rude. Sandra would probably say so. But I didn't really understand what Nate was thinking, because I don't think my parents are bigots. One of my dad's friends from work is gay, and our rabbi is married to another woman. Still, I probably shouldn't have asked him that. Just one more thing on the gigantic list of Things I Shouldn't Have Said.

Luckily, Nate didn't get mad at me. "It's weird," he said while he fiddled with the chain on the swing. "I don't think they'd be angry or bigoted or anything. They love Rabbi Alyssa and Dad's friend Jerry, so I'm pretty sure they're not bigots who just hate all gay people. But I can't totally know how they'll react to ME. And that's hard, you know?"

"Yes," I said. Because I did know, even if it's not exactly the same thing.

"So I don't know for sure what they'll do. And if I don't know for sure, then I guess part of me doesn't want to risk it. Maybe it's not great, but it seems easier that way. Plus . . ."

He didn't finish the sentence. Not at first. I stayed quiet.

". . . plus I just don't want things to change," he continued. "I don't want Mom to do that thing she does where she makes such a big freaking deal out of everything. I don't want to be treated differently. Not like . . ."

He trailed off, and I chewed on the bottom of my lip. Of course I wanted to be a good sister and listen to my brother when he talks to me about Very Important Things. But at first I felt like I was missing something. I just didn't know what. Then, I got it.

"You don't want her treating you like me," I guessed. I wasn't 100% sure that's what he meant, but I had to say it.

Nate's neck turned pink, and after a pause he nodded. "Yeah. That's kind of it. I mean no offense, Viv. Really. But the way she treats you sometimes, like you're some fragile little kid . . ."

"She just wants to protect me." I automatically repeated the thing she's said a million times in the past month. Even though it is seriously annoying and makes no sense at all.

"Sure. But what if I don't want her to protect me

forever?" Nate asked. "What if I just want her to say I'm cool and then back off?"

There wasn't anything I could say to that. Because I totally agree.

I kicked myself off into a swing again. Even though it was quiet, I think my brother and I understood each other very well at that moment.

But now I have a new idea. It's so hard to say everything I want out loud, especially with Mom. I definitely proved that after . . . you know. That Thing.

Well, anyway. What if I tried to tell her how I feel in a letter? Writing letters to you is easier than trying to talk to people with mouth-words. Or at least, it used to be easier. Before you got mad at me.

Ugh, I don't even want to think about THAT. But maybe the letter-writing idea is worth a try.

I wish I could tell you about all this for real but

DRAFT DELETED

Hello. I wanted to talk to you. It feels a little weird to write you a letter when you're just upstairs. But I have so many things to say and I want to try and say them here. I know things haven't gone very well when we talked about important things before, but maybe this will go better. Okay. I'm beginning the letter for real now.

Ugh. I've been staring at this piece of paper for twenty-three minutes. And I still don't know what to say. Writing to VJ is soooo much easier. Or at least it used to be, before I ruined everything.

Right. I'm not supposed to be talking to you about VJ. This is supposed to be a letter about baseball and stuff.

What I want to tell you, Mom, is that I want to play baseball. In games. But you already know that, don't you? You just never listen to me and it doesn't matter if I say it out loud or in a letter or . . .

Never mind. I'll just throw this letter away.

I visited Alex's house today. It had to be today because he has a game tomorrow—lucky! Coach K told me I could come to games and watch if I want, but I don't think I could stand it. If I'm going to a game, I want to play.

Anyway, we practiced throwing in his backyard as usual. I don't want to sound braggy or anything, but I thought my pitches looked pretty good. Alex said so too.

"So, when are you coming back to games?" he asked when we were done pitching. Mrs. Carrillo had brought us lemonade and yummy brownies to eat outside.

For the most part Alex has been pretty nice about not talking about the super-obvious fact that I'm not playing in games, but I guess with the end of the season coming up and everything it's hard to avoid. I took a long sip of my lemonade, but I knew I had to answer him sooner or later.

"I don't know," I told him.

"Uh, no offense, Viv, but why not? You're pitching great, your head looks fine, and oh yeah, by the way, we only have like two other good pitchers on the team. You have to come back!"

Hearing Alex say that I had to come back made me feel good. It really did. But it also made me feel a little sick in my stomach—not like ready-to-puke sick, but definitely not good, either.

"It's hard to explain," I said. I didn't know what else I could say about the whole thing.

Alex sighed. Small brownie chunks trickled down to his chin, and I really wanted to throw him a napkin or something because that is just Bad Manners.

"I know your mom is super-strict, but can't you just talk to her? Or something?"

"I've tried!" I said, then winced. Maybe I wasn't quite yelling, but it was close. And I did not want to yell at Alex, even if he was being kind of annoying at the moment. "Um, sorry. I didn't mean to yell. It's just hard and stuff."

He thumped me on the shoulder. "Hey, that's cool. I don't want to fight. I just want you back in games, you know?"

"I want that too," I said.

After that we just kind of didn't talk about it again. There was a game on TV, so we watched together. Mari came in and she painted my nails during the game. I asked her to do a very light pink color because it's better for pitching.

On the tiny, tiny chance that I ever do get to pitch in games again, I don't want to distract batters with bright nails. It seems unfair to them.

Mari asked a bunch of questions about baseball. Most of them were super-easy, but I tried to do my best and be nice. It went sort of like this:

Mari: So, what does ERA mean?

Alex and me: Earned Run Average.

Mari: Okay, but what does it MEAN?

Alex: I'm not answering your bonkers questions. What're you doing here, anyway?

Mari: I just want to know! Vivy, what does ERA mean?

Me: Um. Well, it's this math thing. It measures how many runs a pitcher gives up on average for every nine innings. That's the length of a game.

Mari: So an ERA of 3 means what, exactly?

Me: It means the pitcher gives up three runs for every nine innings.

Mari: Huh. You're a pretty good teacher. Unlike SOMEONE else I could mention.

That's when Alex stuck his tongue out at her and she flounced out of the room, whipping her long hair behind.

Mari might not know much about baseball, but I think she cares about it at least a little bit. I liked explaining things to her. Which just proves that girls CAN like baseball. I wish I could show that to Mom. Maybe then she'd be okay with me being a ballplayer.

And also . . . I wish that you'd write back to me. I still check my email a bajillion times every day. Hoping that somehow you changed your mind and decided to write me again after all. But I never get anything except for junk mail offering me a FANTASTIC DEAL on tooth whitener strips.

DRAFT DELETED

Vivy,

It's probably rude for me to barge back into your life after everything. But I just can't stop thinking about that email I sent a few weeks ago. I must have drafted other emails back to you a hundred times only to back out of it, but I think I'm going to send this one. For real.

I know I was too harsh and dismissive. I was in a really rough place when I read your email and some of the things you were asking about . . . well, it sent me over the edge. But that doesn't excuse what I did, of course.

Vivy, I messed up. I'm sorry.

I want to go back to the way things were. If it's possible. Maybe it's not.

Your friend (I hope),

VJ

Dear VJ,

Thank you for your letter. I said mean things too. I kept talking about your pitching even when you told me not to. And I am very, very sorry. About all of it.

Okay. I guess we can start talking again.

From,
Vivy

I'm confused. Can we really go back to the way things were before? I want to. But every time I write something to you I know I'll wonder if I'm just being stupid, annoying Vivy again.

It's best just not to bother you at all. You've already given me so much help and it's selfish of me to want more when you are very busy trying to pitch!

Ugh, never mind.

DRAFT DELETED

Good. I'm so glad to hear from you. I handled the whole situation badly, I know. This season has been . . . well, it hasn't gone quite the way I wanted it. To put it mildly.

I'm so interested to hear about everything I missed. How are things with baseball, your family, Alex, and everything else?

I missed talking with you, Vivy. I'm glad we're writing again.

VJ

Things have been going okay, I guess. Practices have been good, but I still can't pitch in games. There are only two and a half weeks left in the season. (Yes, I've been counting.)

I want to pitch! Obviously. But whenever I try to talk to Mom about important things . . . well, bad things happen. So I thought maybe I should try talking to her another way. I tried writing a letter about it instead. Problem was, I couldn't finish it.

I am very, very glad we are writing again. But I don't want to talk too much and just bother you with my problems.

Vivy

Vivy,

You're not bothering me with your problems. Truly.

I am glad to hear that things are going well, but it sounds to me like there's definitely room for improvement. I want you to play in games too—and I think it can happen.

When you write to me, I see so clearly your passion for baseball. I get that your mom is not a baseball person, but I believe you can communicate the important stuff to her. Even if it's not quite in a conventional way. Your idea of writing a letter was a good one. Why not try again?

I realize I might be meddling where I'm not wanted, and I apologize if that's the case. I just want to help you, as you have helped me during these past few months.

Best,

VJ

VJ,

I do want your advice! Of course I do! But I also want to do things by myself and how can I do that and still listen to you? It is Extremely Complicated.

Well, anyway. I thought about it and thought about it until I couldn't stand it anymore. And I . . . I think I'm going to write Mom. And Dad too, because if I'm going to do it, then why not just do all of it.

Wish me luck!
Vivy

I'm sending all the luck-related wishes your way. Let me know how it goes.

VJ

Hi. How are you doing? (I don't know if it's really necessary to include this part, since I just saw you for dinner half an hour ago and I know how you're doing, but I figured I'd better be safe and include all the proper parts of a letter. Just like I learned in social skills group.)

I'm writing to you because I have something very important to say and I don't know how else to say it. I know I messed up before when I tried to talk to you, so I thought I'd try doing it another way.

Mom, I really, really want to play baseball. Not just for practice, but in games. For real.

I know you worry it's not appropriate for me to play, or that I'll get hurt (again). I understand that—really—but I want to say that I'm going to be TWELVE this summer. And next year I'm going to have my bat mitzvah, and maybe that isn't exactly like being a Real Adult like you and Dad, but doesn't it mean something? I think that it should.

I know you're my mom and you want what's best for me. I know you want to protect me. But here's the thing: I want to choose things for myself.

When you tell me I can't do things because I'm a girl or because I'm autistic, it makes me feel really, really lousy. Like I'm less than other people. I know I'm not normal, but I still want to do the things that make me happy. And for me, that's baseball.

You see, there's that moment when one of my knuckle-balls hits Alex's glove with a loud thump and I KNOW it was a strike and the batter knows it too. There isn't anything else in the world like that. And I want to keep feeling it for as long as I can.

I really, really want to pitch again. I'll wear a helmet in the field and do other safety thingies if you want. So, can I?

Love,
Vivy

DEAR DAD,

I sent a letter to Mom. I asked her if I can pitch in real games again. Once she sees that, I'm guessing you guys will talk about it for a really long time and stuff. When you do, will you please stand up for me and say I can pitch? Please please please?

I'm forever grateful to you and Nate and VJ for showing me the wonderfulness of baseball. But when you and Mom talk about ME playing baseball, you let her control things and I don't like it.

I just want to play. And I want you to help me do it.

Love,
Vivy

FROM: VIVIAN JANE COHEN
DATE: JUNE 16
TO: VJ CAPELLO
SUBJECT: JUST SENT THE LETTERS!!!

I just put my letters under the door to Mom and Dad's bedroom. EEEK. VJ, I'm so nervous. What if they say no?

Vivy

Okay, it's done. Now I have to tell you what just happened—which, let me tell you, is BIG. Bigger than big, even.

About an hour after I slipped my letters under the door, Mom called for me. "VIVIAN JANE!"

I peeked out of my room. "Yes?"

That's when Mom told me and Dad to get in the living room for a Very Important Talk. When I got there she held up my letter and waved it in the air.

"Why did you write this, honey?" she asked.

Of course she didn't get it. My heart pounded, and the same old bad feelings boiled up again inside me.

"Because I want to play baseball," I said. I tried not to sound like I was super-annoyed, but I probably did anyway. I mean, I said that in my letter, didn't I? I just could not understand why she asked such a silly question.

"But why did you write a letter about it?" Mom ran a hand through her thick hair. "I'm sorry. I should probably ask that another way. I guess what I meant was, why did you write me a letter instead of talking about it out loud?"

I started twirling the fringe on one of the throw pillows. It's a very thick, plush fringe—exactly what I needed. Halfway through braiding two pieces of fringe together, I drew in a deep breath and tried to find the right words. There was no writing anything down this time.

I had to explain.

"Because . . . because it's easier to say things in a letter," I told her. That's the truth, after all.

Then, a Big Surprise. Dad spoke. "A lot of people on the spectrum find it easier to communicate through writing, Rachel. You know that. Heck, I prefer it. At the office I always send an email instead of making a call if I can get away with it. Usually it works out okay."

Dad gets it. And he understood what I told him in my letter about wanting him to speak up for me! Sometimes I wonder if he's like me—on the spectrum. That would actually explain a lot.

Mom made a scrunched-up face, but she didn't talk right away. That eased the knuckleballs in my stomach a little.

"Yes," I agreed. "Writing is easier. And also . . ."

I hesitated. I knew what I wanted to say, but not how

to say it. I had a feeling that if I said what I really meant it would be Extremely Rude.

"Go on, sweetheart," Dad encouraged. "This is an open-speech zone."

I didn't exactly know what an open-speech zone is, but I figured I might as well say what I think, out loud.

"Also . . . sometimes you don't listen, Mom. But in a letter you HAVE to listen to me."

Her face crumpled. For once she got really, really quiet. The silence stretched out so long I could hardly stand it. Like the moment a ball leaves your hand and you don't know where it's going to end up.

Finally, she said something. "I really had no idea you felt this way, honey. I've only ever wanted to help you show your gifts to the world. For you to have a good life."

"I know," I said, and I really did. I could only hope she understood the other part. That for a good life, I need baseball. Or at least that I want it. A whole lot.

My cheeks flushed, but I tried to ignore it. For once, we were actually talking about something new. This wasn't just another conversation where we kept saying the same things for the thirty gazillionth time.

"You can be just a little overwhelming sometimes," Dad told her. "You're a talker, which is one reason why I fell in love with you. But people like Vivy and me, we need time to find our words. Like when she was young and the speech therapist worked with her to learn how to form words. That challenge didn't go away just because she articulates her speech better now."

"Yes!" I said. "That's why I like writing. I can write to VJ about all sorts of things."

I realized then that Mom might not even know I write to you. I expected her to ask about that, but she didn't. I guess Dad told her. Anyway, for the whole time, she kept very, very quiet.

"I still don't entirely understand how you feel," she admitted at last. "You and I are pretty different. As you know. We worked so hard to help you talk and be comfortable with words when you were younger. It never occurred to me that I might be making it more difficult for you to express yourself now. I'm sorry, honey. And . . . if you ever want to write more letters to me in the future, I'd love to receive them. Really."

I smiled at her.

"I know you're growing up," Mom continued. "And I am so, so proud of everything you're doing with school and your bat mitzvah coming up next year and everything. Vivy, I'm sorry if I don't say it enough, but I really do believe you are becoming an exemplary young woman and I'm proud to be your mom."

All of this felt very good. The only problem was, Mom still hadn't said anything about baseball! Which, hello, is very very important. But she hadn't told me I COULDN'T talk about it. So that's when I decided to ask the Really Important Question: "Can I play in games again?"

Mom let out a long breath and didn't respond right away. That made me feel kind of tight and prickly inside. With a reaction like that there was no way she'd say yes. I knew it.

But then . . .

"Okay," she said finally. "I know you've been waiting very patiently on this. First, I think we should go back to the doctor and make sure there aren't lingering effects from the concussion. But if she says it's okay, then yes. You can play in games—with your batting helmet on, of course."

"Really?" I squealed. I've wanted her to say that for so long. Hearing her finally say the words . . . well, I didn't quite believe it at first.

Mom smiled. "Yes. Really. As your mom, I want what you want. I'm sorry I've forgotten that lately. But I think . . . I think the Flying Squirrels are going to have a great end to the season with you there."

She said that last part with hesitation, like she wasn't quite sure of her own words for once. But they were real. All of it was real.

"Thank you, thank you, thank you!" I said.

I bounced over and wrapped her into a tight hug. That's not usually something I do, but this was a Very Special Moment and I wanted to. Mom grinned wide and drew me in close.

So, I am going to see my doctor tomorrow. And if she says it's okay I will play in games and be a real pitcher again!!!!

Your very, very excited friend,
Vivy

Dear Vivy,

You can't see me, but I am smiling very widely right now. That's excellent news!

In case you don't already know: I'm proud of you. And I can't wait to hear about your upcoming games.

Happily,
VJ

Dear VJ,

So I went to the doctor today and it is official: I can play in games again!

Now I just have to pitch great and show everyone that I deserve to pitch and win games and . . . VJ, this is scary!

Vivy

Vivy,

It's going to be okay. Breathe!

VJ

VJ,

Okay, yes. You're right. Things are good and I want to enjoy it and not get all upset-like again.

When I told Alex I'm coming back to games he pumped his fist and said, "WICKED BEANS!"

(I have no idea how beans can be wicked, though they are very gross. But Alex sometimes says "wicked beans," and I think he means it's good, which it totally is!)

Anyway, that was a very good feeling. When I'm back on the mound and things are scary, I will try to remember what that moment felt like.

Vivy

Dear VJ,

I've pitched a whole bunch of times since the line drive. At practice, at home, at Alex's house. Sometimes I've even pitched to real batters in practice games.

But today, when I went to the park for a game KNOWING that I was going to pitch and it was going to count . . . how could I NOT be at least a little bit scared? Or, well, more than a little?

As I double-knotted my cleats and made sure my ponytail was tied the right way, I just kept thinking about that boy. The one who hit the line drive that hit me. I knew logically that what happened wasn't his fault. He was just trying to hit the ball. He wasn't aiming for my head.

I knew that. Really.

My hands still trembled while I sat on the bench. Just waiting to pitch.

Marty started the game. He didn't do very well, giving

up four runs in three innings. That meant Coach K called me in to start the fourth. We were already behind, 4–1. But maybe, just maybe, I could help the team get back into it.

When the game started I put my Pitching Face up. I told myself I would NOT worry about being hit in the head. I would just pitch.

The first batter popped up on the second pitch and I started to feel the knots in my stomach loosen a little bit. Maybe I could beat these boys.

Then the next batter came up to the plate. Even worse: A gigantic boy came into the on-deck circle. He was so big and tough-looking that he reminded me of THAT boy. The one who hit me.

I know you're supposed to focus on the hitter who is at the plate, not the one in the on-deck circle. Coach K always preaches going one batter at a time and all that. But, well, the boy who looked just like the one who hit me was in the on-deck circle! Getting ready to hit against me. How was I supposed to just pretend that wasn't happening, VJ? I couldn't do it.

The first pitch I threw didn't knuckle, not even a little bit. It flew right into the batter's shoulder. He tried to duck, but he couldn't, and I felt pretty bad about it. That meant it was called a hit-by-pitch and THAT meant a runner on first base. Leaving me to face the gigantic boy.

Alex trotted up to the mound for a Talk. "Viv, you totally can own this guy," he said. "You just gotta throw the knuckle like in practice."

Right then I could barely remember how to pitch at all. Let alone all the fancy stuff you told me about my hips and release point and stuff. But I told Alex okay and shooed him back to the plate.

While Alex headed back to the plate, the gigantic boy took a few big practice swings in the batter's box. Was he trying to intimidate me? Because it totally worked.

Next, I threw him three straight pitches that nearly scraped the dirt. Now the count was three balls and no strikes. Pitching to him still scared me, a lot. As you can probably tell. But I knew in my heart that walking a batter is a coward's way out, so I decided I wouldn't do it.

My next pitch went right out over the plate. And he drove it over the left fielder's head for a home run.

It's strange, but as I watched the ball fly out of reach, I thought, well, at least the ball didn't hit me. At least I was still safe. Such a cowardly thought, I know, but it's the truth.

I bet you've never had such a terrible thought after giving up a home run.

After that, things only got worse. I gave up another two runs before Coach K finally pulled me out of the game. He didn't say anything. I guess there wasn't anything to be said.

VJ, do you know that movie about girls playing baseball? The team manager character played by Tom Hanks says, "There's no crying in baseball."

That's a good rule. But I never realized it would be so hard to follow.

Once Coach K told me I was done for the day, I plopped down on the far end of the bench. Our hitters scored a few runs, but I couldn't really pay attention to anything that happened out on the field. I stared into the swirly wood pattern in the bench. I couldn't even think about baseball—it just hurt too much. Tears prickled at the corner of my eye and I just knew that if I let myself think about what happened they'd come pouring out and it would never, ever stop.

Alex came over and tried to cheer me up, but I couldn't get any words out. He eventually shrugged and walked away. The others stayed clear of me too. At that moment, aloneness was a wonderful gift. Too bad a certain jerk of a pitcher wouldn't let me enjoy it for long.

Kyle sat down right next to me in the fourth inning.

"Rough game, Viv," he taunted.

As usual, Kyle kept his voice real quiet. I hated him calling me Viv like Alex does.

"What, you're not chatty today?" he said after I stayed silent. "Too bad. I was wondering what pathetic excuse you'd come up with this time. 'I'm Vivy and I can't pitch to the big scary boy because I had mush for brains even before I got hit in the head.'"

While he talked he put on this fake high-pitched voice and crammed his words together so it sounded all funny. I do not talk like that, VJ, I do not!

"Go away," I said.

"Oh, it can speak after all. Too bad it can't pitch." He scooted closer to me. Soon I felt the hot puff of his breath attacking my face. "The league is figuring out your little trick, monkey-girl. It's only a matter of time till my dad sees you're a waste. And then you'll be gone."

He went away after that, but as I watched him go my cheeks dampened with awful, traitor tears. So I guess there is crying in baseball after all.

From,
Vivy

As much as I enjoy *A League of Their Own*, that line is horse manure (if you'll excuse my language). If you don't have emotions on the baseball field, then you don't care enough.

I'd prefer to keep this between us, but I've cried because of baseball a few times. First when I shredded up my shoulder in the minors. The doctor told me I'd probably never pitch again and . . . well, I was a grown man of 23, but I sobbed like a little kid who got his very favorite toy taken away.

Then I cried again last October. I guess you know why.

There's not much I can say to comfort you after a start like that. But I wish you all the best in the next game.

VJ

Thanks. That helps, a little bit. I don't know. It's been a whole day since my start and I can't stop thinking about it. At breakfast today Nate had to tell me to pass the cereal box at least three times before I realized what was going on. Mom gave a Very Big Frown and I know she's wondering if letting me go back was a mistake. I hate it, VJ, I really do.

"Stop moping," Nate told me at breakfast this morning. "Get ready for next time instead."

I didn't respond—I just stuck my tongue out at him.

He's probably right, though. Ugh.

Vivy

So today I pitched again. This time it was a little less stinky. I pitched two innings and gave up only one earned run. But VJ, it just didn't feel very good. There was this awful tingling all over me—all over my neck, on the insides of my stomach. And of course, in my fingertips. And how can I possibly throw a decent knuckleball with all of THAT going on inside me?

I wanted so much to play in games again and I still do, but . . . why does it all have to be so hard?

Vivy

Dear Vivy,

If you ever figure out the answer to that question, let me know. My own recent starts have been, in a word, stinky (as you would say!). The other guys on my team ask me about it and I just don't know what I'm supposed to say. If I'm being perfectly honest, I don't know how to talk about it without screaming. I can't even think about it without feeling the very, very strong urge to do just that.

Sorry I can't be of greater assistance to you. But I'm certainly here to commiserate.

VJ

I like the word "commiserate." I wasn't sure what it meant, so I looked it up. Now I know it means to share misery. And that is definitely what we've been doing lately.

I really hope it's okay to say this, but I am very sorry that you had another hard start. I will let you know if I figure out the secret to pitching well all the time. (Well, okay, that probably doesn't exist. But it's nice to imagine, isn't it?)

Also, I didn't mention this in my last email, but something happened with Alex after the game and I have feelings about it but I'm not 100% sure what they are.

"Um, Viv?" Alex said. "You know I think you're great and all that, but you really need to trust me more."

"I trust you," I said. "You're my best friend."

Then I immediately wondered if that was the right thing to say. It's true, of course, but I also didn't know if it's okay to tell someone that they are your best friend. Especially if you don't know if YOU are THEIR best friend too.

The moment after I said it seemed to last for a really long time, even though it probably wasn't very long at all.

"Duh, yeah," he said. "You're my best friend too. I meant more that you have to trust me on the mound. Ya know?"

The part where he said I'm his best friend was super-awesome, but I couldn't relax. Not really. I crossed my arms over my chest and stared at his chin. Not his eyes. "What do you mean?" I asked.

"Ever since you came back to playing games, you, like, never throw a fastball! Even when I call for it a million times, you just go knuckleball, knuckleball, knuckleball. If I'm gonna be your catcher, you need to trust my calls."

I knew he was right, but VJ, I just get so scared about throwing my fastball. It isn't fast! How can I possibly throw my not-fast fastball to all those gigantic batters? I really don't understand why he keeps calling fastballs when I'm not very good at throwing them.

Besides, you know that one line drive that hit me in the head and almost ruined everything forever? I don't know if you remember, but VJ, that pitch was a fastball.

I tried explaining everything to him. "My fastball just isn't good. I can't throw it every time you want me to," I said.

"Uh, yeah, actually you can. Remember what VJ said: The speed difference messes with batters' timing. So you can mow 'em down with the fastball even if it isn't really the fastest. Um, wait. Is it okay for me to talk about VJ? You're not going to bite me like the last time, are you? Please don't bite me, Viv, not after I just spent half an hour crouched behind the plate trying to catch your bonkers pitch. That would just be cruel and unusual punishment."

"You can talk about VJ," I said. "But I don't know about the fastball thing."

"You don't have to throw it ALL the time. But at least think about it, 'kay?"

"Okay," I said.

I kept my promise to him and I have been thinking about it. But I'm just not sure I can trust my fastball. I mean, I barely can trust my knuckleball most days!

Baseball is hard, VJ. But I guess you already know that.

Vivy

Dear Vivy,

As pitchers, we have to trust so many people. Our catchers, our fielders, our coaches. Knuckleballers have to trust even more than other pitchers. We're usually not big strikeout guys, so we just have to have faith that the fielders behind us will catch the ball when we need them to. It's not always easy. Don't tell anyone I said this, but even now, after years of professional baseball and a Cy Young Award, I hold my breath every time I hear the bat crack. I generally like to be in control of things. But when the batter makes contact, it's all (quite literally) out of my hands. And part of me just can't stand it, even after all these years.

Plus, if all that weren't enough, there's the other stuff. The stuff that really shouldn't impact the game, but it does anyway. I'm one of two knuckleballers in all of MLB, and one guy on a rather short list of Black American starting pitchers. It's hard not to feel like my success (or lack thereof) will impact others too. I guess you might feel similarly.

So, yes, it is hard. But Alex isn't just any old person. He's proven himself to be not only a steadfast friend, but a skilled catcher too. He knows you, Vivy—as a pitcher and as a person.

So . . . give the fastball a try?

VJ

FROM: VIVIAN JANE COHEN

DATE: JUNE 25

TO: VJ CAPELLO

RE: TRUST, BASEBALL, AND OTHER HARD THINGS

Thanks for the advice.

I talked to Alex and we worked out a deal. If he calls a fastball, I can shake it off once, but the next time he signals it, I throw it. That's pretty scary, but I guess the worst thing that can happen is my fastball gets hit. And I can live with that. I think. If you can keep going out there after a rough game then so can I.

Sorry, I didn't mean to bring up your pitching. I know that's bad. I won't won't won't do it again.

In happier things, something really great happened! It was yesterday, when Dad and me were driving home from baseball practice. Usually our drive home is pretty quiet. Not the awful, uncomfortable kind of silence but the cozy sort. We don't need to say much to each other. But this time, he did say things.

"Not to get too sappy or anything, but I have to say that I am so, so proud of you," he said. "I was a little worried about how you'd do, coming back to baseball. But you've done well. Just like I knew you could."

I bounced a little in my seat. "Thanks," I told him. "But I still haven't won a game."

He laughed. "Patience, my little flying squirrel! Did you know that VJ Capello didn't win a game until his sixth major-league start?"

Of course I knew that already. I nodded. (Actually, I do have a question about this, VJ. When you made those first five starts and didn't get a single win . . . did it feel like you never would?)

"Your win is coming. I'll bet Coach K starts you in one of the last few games," he said.

"Not if Kyle is pitching," I mumbled.

"Kyle, the coach's son? He's pretty good. But he can't start every game, and you're way better than that Marty kid."

I laughed a little, then felt bad about it. I mean, it's not Marty's fault that he isn't very good at pitching. Laughing at him for that is something Kyle would do, and I don't want to be like him at all. Even if he CAN pitch.

Since Dad seemed to be in a pretty good mood and everything, I decided maybe it was okay to ask a Very Important Question. "Dad, why don't you talk to Mom about stuff?"

His eyebrows jerked up into his Surprised Face. "You're

going to have to be a little more specific. I talk to your mother about plenty of things."

I clenched my teeth together and started to twirl a thick strand of hair around my finger. Sometimes Dad can be very, very annoying.

"You know what I mean!" I said. "Why don't you tell her not to be so . . . Mom? You know, with letting me play baseball and stuff."

Dad laughed again, but this time it was his nervous laugh. For a long time, he didn't say anything and I squirmed in my seat. I felt certain I'd just made a Very Bad Mistake.

"You're right," he said finally. "I have let her make a lot of the big decisions when it comes to you."

"But why?" I really, really didn't want to be rude or anything, but I had to know.

"It's pretty complicated," Dad said. His hands clutched the steering wheel harder than normal.

"I can understand complicated things!"

"Yes, you can." Dad let out a looong breath. "Okay. I'll try to explain. You know . . . when I was younger, I had a lot of problems that are similar to yours."

"Mmm-hmm," I said. Because duh, I already kind of knew that. I wanted to know more. I needed to know more.

"Back then, they didn't really have a name for it," he

continued. "People just made assumptions about me, and life could be, well, pretty hard at times. And I guess I just didn't want you to have bad experiences like I did. So I turned some things over to your mom. I thought she'd know how to handle all the social stuff better than me."

"Oh." I twirled my hair some more and thought about it for a while. "That doesn't make very much sense. But I understand. I think."

Dad laughed—this time for real. "Honey, I think you are absolutely right. I'll try to keep that in mind."

So that is another Very Good Thing!

You know, I wouldn't have thought that my DAD still felt so many things from when he was a kid himself. I mean, I never even think of him being a kid like me, even though Grandma Beth loves to show me all these old pictures of him. But I guess dads don't forget the things that happened before they were dads.

Now I feel pretty okay about things with my parents.

If only . . . if only I could feel like that on the mound, too.

Vivy

Dear Vivy,

I am very glad to hear that you and your parents have reached a greater understanding. That's huge.

To answer your question about the beginning of my career: Yes, of course it was stressful to not win a single game in my first five starts! Even though I had a good record in the minor leagues, when something like that happens it's easy to start thinking that maybe you'll never win a single game. That everything you sacrificed for this sport—all the long road trips to small towns in Texas with 105-degree weather in August, the sore arms and countless physical therapy sessions—were for nothing. Plus, I'm an old Black knuckleballer. So there was always that other question: Do they really believe I can do this? Or are they going to give my spot away to some young kid who lights up the radar gun?

It is completely normal to feel disappointed when things don't quite happen on the field the way you imagine them in your head. I know. But I still believe in you.

Your friend,
VJ

Thank you for telling me about your first games and stuff. It helps to know that you think and feel the same kinds of things I do.

Now I want to tell you about something super-cool that just happened.

Nate ran in twenty minutes after we already started eating, which earned him a Mom-glare. "And where have you been, Nathan?" she asked.

"Practice," he mumbled. Which I knew was a total lie.

Nate didn't speak much after that because he was stuffing his face with mashed potatoes. (My mom is a very good cook, if you were wondering.)

Even though his cheeks were all puffy with mashed potatoes, there was something funny about his face. I couldn't quite identify it, but I just knew he was thinking about Very Important Things.

"Actually . . ." Nate began to talk, then stopped. Mom and Dad both looked at him. But they didn't say anything either.

Finally, more Nate-words came. "Actually, I wasn't at practice. Not exactly."

I was pretty sure it's not possible to be not-exactly at practice. I mean, duh. More important, though, I thought I knew what Nate wanted to say next. And I knew it was a Very Big Deal.

He glanced over at me, and I smiled extra-wide. I hope that helped him, at least a little.

Mom still didn't say anything through all of this. She really has been different lately. Not quite so talky. It's nice.

"I wasn't at practice," Nate repeated. "I was hanging out with a guy on my team. His name's Tyler and he's my boy-friend. I'm gay."

His voice got a little shaky at the end. But he still said everything.

"So, yeah," he said. "That's what's going on. I just wanted to tell you."

That's when Mom did a really, really cool thing. She put down her fork, marched around the kitchen table, and pulled Nate into a super-tight hug. And that is totally the best kind of hug. Nate's eyebrows bounced around during all that. Still, I could tell from his silly grin that he liked it.

When Mom FINALLY let Nate go, Dad spoke. "Thanks so much for telling us. So, when can we meet Tyler?"

"Soon," Nate answered. I noticed then that his eyes were

kind of watery, though he didn't seem sad at all. He looked at Mom, then back at Dad. "I'll bring him over. But you are not allowed to embarrass me in front of him, okay? No stories about my first T-ball game or the time I put M&Ms up my nose or anything else that happened before I turned ten. All of that is 100% off-limits. In fact, maybe you guys just shouldn't say more than one sentence at a time. That sounds fair."

"No promises, kid," Dad replied.

Nate groaned, but not for real. He was still grinning really wide.

"I won't embarrass you in front of your boyfriend," I promised him.

"Thank you, Vivy. Maybe I should just introduce you to Tyler and leave it at that."

Of course Mom protested and Dad promised to be not-embarrassing and then after dinner we ate the most yummiest cheesecake that Mom had been hiding in the back of the refrigerator for a special day.

I'd say that makes for a Very Good Day.

And speaking of good things . . . the game is coming up in a few minutes. Your game. I know I've said this before, but I have a good feeling about this one, VJ.

Vivy

Dear Vivy,

There is much to write about in this letter, so please forgive me for being long-winded. I have a lot to say. And I want to say it to you.

By now I'm sure you watched my own trial yesterday. What an exhausting, exhilarating game THAT was.

Going into it, I knew I had to pitch well. My manager can't keep giving me the ball if I can't put up some strong starts. And of course I've heard the rumblings from sports radio, and even from the other guys on the team. That meant my nerves were high from the very start.

Then I gave up four runs in the first inning, thanks to a combination of bad pitching and two infield errors. Yes, I know. I shouldn't dwell on the errors. I keep telling you that you need to trust your teammates. But when my shortstop made that terrible throw, I felt something very, very close to rage.

"Sorry, VJ!" he called.

I knew he meant well. Still, I ground my teeth. Sorry? He was sorry? I was the one who would have to deal with the consequences of his mistake! When I already had so much to prove.

With every run that crossed home plate that inning, my hope abandoned me little by little. This was the nightmare I've been living all season. I know what I need to do, but whenever I actually throw the ball I freeze up at the last second. Because I just keep remembering that terrible moment from last year's Series. I keep needing to make up for it. And my stiff, scared fingers can't throw right.

On most days, the manager would have taken me out of the game after the leadoff double in the second. But our bullpen got hammered in a blowout loss the night before, so there wasn't much of a choice. This was just going to be one of those days when I needed to carry the team.

My catcher came up to the mound to give me a breather and—quite deservedly—a lecture. He used rather colorful language in English and Spanish both.

Still, I wasn't entirely focused on what he was saying. Instead, I thought about you. About the faith you have in me, even if I don't always deserve it. I thought about all the supposedly smart things I've said to you about focusing on the next pitch and trusting your catcher and all that. Yet I myself have failed to do that time and time again this season.

"I'll do better," I found myself saying. "I'll fix this, even if that means having to strike out every batter myself. I'll do it."

My catcher just looked at me, his face full of so much sympathy that I ached.

"*Oye, pana*. You don't need to strike out every guy," my catcher said. "You have a whole team here. Now you're going to start pitching like you again and you don't have to do it by yourself. *Sí?*"

As he spoke, I could feel an invisible weight being lifted up off my shoulders—not all of it, but enough. For the first time since last October, I really felt like maybe I did have a team behind me. Supporting me.

There wasn't much time to relish the feeling. I had a game to pitch, after all.

I went back to the rubber.

By some minor miracle, I got out of the second inning unscathed. Then I pitched another scoreless inning, and then I did it again, and again, until at last I was finishing up the seventh inning. After my manager clapped me on the back and told me "good job," I looked up at the scoreboard for the first time in two hours. That's when I realized I was in line for the win.

Although that game hardly counts as one of the best

performances of my career, I must say it was one of the most satisfying.

Every single teammate and coach came up to congratulate me after it was all over. It shouldn't have surprised me. But it did.

Ever since then, I've been thinking about some things. The things we've talked about in our letters, and things we haven't talked about so much.

For all this time you've been forthcoming with me, but I've given you only small pieces of myself. I've doled out pitching advice like some kind of knuckleball sage, but I haven't really been honest about me.

So, let me tell you a story. You already know this one, but bear with me.

Last year, my team made it to the World Series. This event, obviously, was a big deal. Very few of us had ever been to the Series before. Maybe some of us would never make it back again.

This was it: Our chance to fulfill a dream cherished since we were boys playing Little League. Those seven games were everything.

We played pretty well in the Series, winning three games out of the first six. In no small part, our success was thanks to me. The oddball pitcher who couldn't throw harder than 80 miles per hour.

I wasn't scheduled to start Game 7, since I already started two other games and won both of them. But I knew I might have to go in and pitch in relief. To try and win it all.

It happened in the eleventh inning, during a tie game at the other team's ballpark. Every single person in that stadium was rooting against me, but I didn't care. I knew with complete certainty I could win it. I could be a hero. If we won this game, if I won the game, we'd win the Series. If not, well . . . I didn't even want to consider it.

Except. On my very first pitch I threw a knuckleball that didn't knuckle. I might have been able to get away with it on some other day, but not that one. The batter—an utterly mediocre player with a career .273 batting average—pounded it over the fence for a home run. Game over. Dream over. Not just for me, but for 24 other guys, too.

No one remembered how well I'd done in my other games. To be honest with you, I barely remembered it myself. I only knew the foul taste of defeat—yes, defeat has a taste. It's lurked in my mouth ever since that pitch sailed over my head. Only last night did the foulness start to leave me.

Ever since then, I've been consumed by the feeling that I had to fix it. That only I could fix it. But I realized something on the mound last night, while I listened to my catcher and thought about all the things you've said to me. I realized that I was wrong.

Maybe I don't need to do everything all by myself. Maybe I can count on other people to have my back—yes, even when my shortstop makes a bad throw.

It's easy to tell someone else to focus on the next pitch and trust her catcher. Doing it yourself is much harder. But I'd like to give it a try.

Thank you, Vivy, for giving me this opportunity to think about these things and for listening to my ramblings.

Now, enough about me! I know you have your own games coming up, and I can't wait to hear all about it.

VJ

VJ,

I knew it! I knew you'd pitch great and you did and I'm just SO SO SO happy for you. You were totally amazing!

Also, thank you for telling me all that stuff. You didn't have to, but you did. I am sooooo happy to be your friend.

I have a game coming up too—the last game of the season. The game is tomorrow, actually. Coach K says I'm the starting pitcher. It's all very exciting and very scary!

If I mess up, I won't get another chance until next year. If I even get to come back next year.

But right now, I have to think good thoughts. Okay, I'm thinking good thoughts starting now.

Vivy

Dear VJ,

I know I'm supposed to be thinking good thoughts. But I looked at the schedule and found out the scariest thing. Our last game of the season, the one I'm going to start TODAY, is against the Seabirds. The last time I started a game against the Seabirds, I ended up in the hospital. Now I have to pitch against them AGAIN. Eek.

I really did try to get a good night's sleep last night, because Coach K says that is Very Important. But every time I closed my eyes, I saw that ball zooming toward me.

There was no way I could just drift off into a peaceful sleep.

Sometimes when I have trouble sleeping, I like to gulp down a nice glass of milk. I don't know if it actually helps, but at least I'm doing something that isn't just tossing around in my bed. So I crept down the stairs to get my milk.

When I reached the bottom, the lights from the living room nearly blinded me. I wasn't the only one who couldn't get to sleep.

"Hey, Vivy," Dad said. He was hunched over his laptop, but looked up when I entered the room. "Trouble sleeping?"

I nodded, and he waved for me to join him on the couch. I curled myself up into a ball next to him and for several long moments, neither of us said anything.

Finally Dad spoke. "So. You want to tell me what has you in the Cohen family insomnia club tonight?"

I pulled at the loose threads shooting up from the couch cushion. "The Seabirds," I said.

"Ah," Dad said. "Those boys. Well, I have a feeling that this next start is going to go better for you."

"It can't exactly go any worse than the last one," I mumbled.

Dad gave me a pat on the arm. "Yeah. I know it's been rough. But maybe things will finally go your way tomorrow," he said.

"Maybe," I said.

But I didn't really believe it, and Dad gave me one of his looks. "You don't seem terribly convinced, hon."

I fidgeted with my fingers and tried to come up with a smart explanation for him. "With everything that happened last time, how can I possibly think that things will go well this time?"

"You can't," Dad replied immediately. "There are no guarantees in baseball. But that's where hope comes in. It never hurts to hope."

Hope. It's such a funny word—short, but with a definite kick. I tried to feel hope, and I think I sort of did. At least a little bit.

"Okay," I whispered. "I'll try to hope."

Then I went and poured myself a glass of milk. I drank all of it in a single gulp. Since I fell asleep the moment I got back into bed, I guess it worked.

But when I woke up this morning and tried to feel that feeling of hope again . . . I just couldn't.

Wish me luck, VJ.

Vivy

Vivy,

You don't need my luck. But I'm rooting for you.

Hopefully,
VJ

FROM: VIVIAN JANE COHEN
DATE: JUNE 28
TO: VJ CAPELLO
SUBJECT: THE GAME

Today was it. The last game of the season. My last chance to prove I can be a real pitcher.

No one actually said, "No baseball for you next year if you pitch badly today!" But I felt it anyway. I couldn't not.

Everything was so hot, VJ. Even with short sleeves the jersey weighed heavy on my chest. The sunlight burned against my eyes and skin. My batting helmet could only do so much to protect me.

When I got to the field and saw the swarm of Seabird-turquoise uniforms, I got so distracted that I tripped over my own cleats. I knocked into Benny the center fielder by mistake. "Watch it, Cohen," he said. But he wasn't really mean about it.

Since it was a home game, the bench felt nice and familiar. I flapped my fingers while I settled into my usual spot. In the minutes before the game started, I tried counting backward from 100 like Dr. Reeve says I should whenever things get to be too much. As I concentrated on the numbers, the Seabirds and their bats and muscles faded from my mind.

Before I jogged up to take the mound, Alex called out to me. "Remember: We've got a deal here. You throw a fast-ball at least half the time when I call for it. And believe me, you don't wanna know what I have planned for you if you break our deal."

He wiggled his eyebrows at me, so I knew he was kidding. Still, I knew I had to keep my end of our bargain. The thought of throwing my not-fast fastballs made me feel a little sick, but I promised Alex I'd do it. And I always keep my promises.

When I stepped onto the mound, I smiled. Even with all the scariness, this was still exactly the place I wanted to be.

Alex called a fastball on the first pitch. Geez, he really does not kid around!

The voice in my head screamed at me, but I kept my promise. I threw the fastball. And the batter just took the pitch for a strike, no big deal. Maybe I really could do this.

That first batter hit a weak grounder on my third pitch, a knuckleball. The second baseman fielded it with no problem.

Batter number two hit a soft line drive to center field. Benny flashed me a thumbs-up after he made the catch. My lips tugged upward into a teeny-tiny smile.

Then, That Boy came up to the plate. The one who hit me with a line drive. He was just as big as ever, of course—maybe even bigger.

I stared at him while he took a few powerful practice swings in the batter's box. Maybe it was all part of his plan to scare me. Maybe that's just what he does to get ready. It didn't matter. I clenched my fists and told myself that this boy was not, not, NOT going to bother me. Not today.

Alex called for another first-pitch fastball, and I glared at him. Sure, we had a deal. But did he really have to call so many of them?

But I remembered Alex asking me if I trusted him. I remembered you saying that a great knuckleball pitcher needs to trust her catcher. And I threw another fastball.

That Boy fouled it straight back. I let out a humongous breath when the ball thunked up against the metal cage.

On the next pitch, Alex signaled for a knuckleball like usual. My knuckleball knuckled, and the boy swung straight through it. Strike two.

The next pitch plummeted into the dirt, bringing the count to 1-2. I flapped my glove hand up against my hip and tried to breathe kind-of-sort-of normally. I could still do this.

I clutched the ball in a knuckleball grip and released it. My fingers knew as soon as the ball left my hand that it was a knuckle-y one. I didn't even need to watch it flutter toward the plate.

VJ, the boy swung straight through the air. That made one strikeout for me, and I'd made it through the inning without giving up a single hit!

Coach K nodded at me as I took my seat on the bench. After all this time I've gotten used to his nods and I think this one meant "Good. Now do it again."

Right. I wasn't nearly done. Not yet.

Our team scored two runs in our half of the inning, so I practically danced out to the mound for the top of the second. My knuckle knuckled, my fastball whizzed as much as it ever does, and I allowed exactly zero runs. The TV announcers would've said, "Vivy Cohen is LOCKED IN today, folks."

Even though I gave up my first hit in the third inning, I managed to get out of it okay. By then the score was Flying Squirrels 4, Seabirds 0. (Don't you just love the way the number 0 looks—all nice and round? I sure do, especially when it's me putting up the zeros!)

Things got harder in the fourth. I gave up a single to the first batter. Then, That Boy came up to the plate—again.

Alex signaled for a break and raced up to the mound. "The batters after this dude are kinda not great. You want to intentionally walk him?"

Maybe that would've been the smart thing to do. Probably it would have been the smart thing to do. But I wasn't about to let That Boy just get on base without a fight. I said, "No way."

Alex broke into a really big grin. "Wicked beans! I just wanted to give you the choice in case you wanted it."

"Well, I don't," I told him. "I'm pitching to this guy."

Even though I talked tough, I have to say I didn't exactly feel 100% confident. My fingers didn't quite grip the ball right, and the first pitch was not very knuckle-y.

The boy pulled his bat backward, then drove it forward before I could blink. For a second I was sure sure sure that the ball was going to hit me in the head. Just like that other game.

Instead, it soared right over my head and into the outfield. The runner at first base took off and I just knew it—I wasn't going to get my shutout today. I flapped my hand through my glove and tried to wish away the sinking lump of disappointment in my stomach.

By the time Benny fished the ball up from the grass, the runner had slid into home and That Boy made it to third base standing up. So maybe I should've walked him after all.

Even though I felt sweaty all over, I could practically hear you telling me, in that nice way of yours, that I still needed to focus on the next batter. Put it all behind me. So that's exactly what I tried to do.

I wish I could give you a play-by-play recap of everything that happened after that, but I don't remember all the exact details. Here's what I do know: I got one out, and then another one, and then somehow another one until I was done with the inning and Alex grinned real wide at me.

My final game: four innings pitched, three hits, no walks, and one earned run allowed.

Even better, my whole family was there to see me pitch! I tried not to think about it too much during the actual game, but when Coach K gave me a pat on the back and took away the ball for the last time I glanced over to the stands. All three of them stood up and cheered for me. Yes, even Mom. That felt really good—almost as good as what Coach K said to me at the very end: "Good job, Cohen."

We won the game by a score of 5–2, and the Flying Squirrels now have an even record for the season. 10 wins, 10 losses. Also, I know you're not supposed to care that much about individual achievements, but since we won the game that made ME the winning pitcher. Can you believe it, VJ?!!! Coach K thinks I'm the first girl ever to win a game in our league. But honestly, I don't really care if I'm the first or 385th.

I just want to pitch next season.

After the game ended, Coach K took all of us to Moe's Pizza in downtown Lakeview. I was a little nervous about this, because Moe's is dark and noisy, plus it always smells like pepperoni grease. But I liked eating pizza—sausage and extra cheese for me—and hanging out with the rest of the team. Still, after a while all the people talking and singing victory songs felt like too much, so I escaped for the bathroom. Just for a few minutes of nice quietness.

One thing about Moe's: It doesn't have separate bathrooms for boys and girls. There's only one. And when I got in line for it Kyle was just standing there, leaning up against the brick wall all smug-like. Ugh ugh ugh.

I hoped maybe he'd just be happy with the win and yummy pizza. Maybe he wouldn't feel like he just HAD to be mean again. But, well, no such luck.

"Hey, monkey-girl. Are you really coming back next year? I thought for sure you'd switch to softball. Or the Special Olympics," Kyle said.

He made a sneering face and I could feel the walls of the pizza shop closing in on me. The TVs squawking and glasses clinking and people yelling got louder and louder.

"Still not talking, huh?" he mocked. "Oh, come on. I know you can talk. Well, sort of."

I thought about it. Adults always say don't respond to

bullies. Don't stoop to their level. But I've been TRYING not to stoop to Kyle's level all season! And it just hasn't worked at all.

That's when I decided I needed to say something. And for once, I knew exactly the right words.

"I don't care how many notes or gum balls you give me. I'm playing next year," I told him. Even though I wasn't completely sure Coach K wanted me back on the team, I figured I might as well say it. Let him get used to the idea. "What, are you scared I'll take away your spot as number one starter?"

His jaw dropped straight down like one of those toy puppets. "As if you ever could!" he snapped after a long pause.

Still, I knew I'd gotten to him. For the first and probably last time ever. So I forced my mouth into making one of those fake-smiles that Kyle loves so much. "You know, I can teach you the knuckleball grip if you want to learn another pitch," I offered. Really, I could not believe my own nerve. "Maybe that will help you."

Kyle stared at me with big eyes and said some really bad words. I sucked in a breath, worrying that maybe I'd gone too far with it.

But you know what? After that he turned away and ignored me.

Now that I think about it, though, it is kind of weird that he reacted like that. Is he ACTUALLY scared I'll take his place as number one pitcher?

That is totally bonkers-bananas!

Anyway, after I came back from the bathroom, I slid into my seat next to Alex.

"I told you that the fastball would work!" he said.

"You were right," I told him.

"Of course I was. Catchers are always right."

I smiled at him. "If you say so."

"Well, I do."

Then we talked about the game some more. Well, mostly it was Alex talking while I listened. But that was fine by me. The only problem was that while Alex gave his play-by-play recap of everything that happened, one tiny annoying thought started wriggling itself into my brain.

What if the team didn't want me again next year? That would make this my last game ever.

Logically I knew that Coach K probably wanted me back. But probably wasn't good enough for me. I needed a definitely.

That not-knowing feeling was awful and distracting. So I took a deep breath and made myself walk over to Coach K.

"Can I come back next year?" I blurted out.

He looked at me, the lines of his face screwed up all funny. My heart pattered.

"Huh? Oh, yeah. Come back next year. We're going to need one of our best pitchers."

One of our best pitchers. ME. That's what he said!

I flapped my fingers so hard right then, VJ. And I didn't even try to hide it. Because I pitched well today. Because I am going to pitch again next year. And because now I have Alex and you and Coach K and Mom and Dad and Nate and BASEBALL. Always baseball.

VJ, I don't know if I can be the first girl in the major leagues. That's all a really long way off and I have a lot to do until then and stuff. But for now I will keep throwing knuckleballs. And they are going to be very, very knuckle-y.

Your friend,
Vivy

Acknowledgments

I didn't realize until publishing this book that writing, like baseball, is a team sport, but it is.

I must begin by expressing my love and thanks to my husband, Neil, for always being my first reader. I don't know if I could have done this if you hadn't said "awesome!" four years ago when I first said I wanted to write a novel.

Thank you to Mom, Dad, and my sister, Emily, for always believing that I could be a writer even when I didn't believe it myself.

I am so fortunate to have a completely supportive family: my grandfather Charles Pripas, aunt Edith Dorsen, in-laws Wynn Kapit and Laurie Hanson, and honorary family member Jayne Carlin. Thanks to each and every one of you for your love and support.

Much thanks to my agent Jennifer Udden, for your unwavering enthusiasm about Vivy and her story. You really found the perfect home for her. Thanks also to Tricia Ready for your kindness and assistance.

My editor, Dana Chidiac, understands Vivy's story as well as I could have hoped and has done so much to help me bring it to life. Since the first time we spoke, her insightful comments and questions have helped me make this book stronger. Thank you for making my debut experience a great one, and for being cool about my 2,000-word emails discussing edits. Thanks also to the rest of the All-Star team at Dial and Penguin Young Readers: Lauri Hornik, Nancy Mercado, Regina Castillo, Tabitha Dulla, Cerise Steel, Emily Romero, Christina Colangelo, Carmela Iaria, Kaitlin Kneafsey, Debra Polansky, and everyone else who touched this book.

Vivienne To has created a beautiful illustration that perfectly captures Vivy and her world. So many thanks to her and cover designer Theresa Evangelista.

Many friends in the autistic community and neurodiversity movement have supported me over the years, and without them this book would not exist. I'd like to particularly thank Ari Ne'eman for listening to me talk about the process of writing this book (and everything else). Shannon des Roches Rosa and Phil Schwarz kindly helped me make sure that I got Vivy's parents right.

Sam Hawk and Isaac Fitzsimons offered brilliant comments about Nate's and VJ's experiences respectively, for which I am so thankful. I take full responsibility for any shortcomings.

Adrianna Cuevas, thank you for reading this book and many others in various forms! Your encouragement has helped me on many, many occasions.

Mike Grosso mentored me through revising this book in Pitch Wars 2017, and the book is much better for his thoughtful ideas. Thank you for believing in me and in Vivy!

A big thanks to all of the 2017 Pitch Wars mentees, with a special shout-out to Rachel Simon, Landon Spencer, and Arianne Costner. Thanks to Brenda Drake for everything you do to make Pitch Wars a great program.

The Author Mentor Match program has also been huge for my development as a writer. Thank you, Gail Villanueva, for believing in my abilities and taking the time to help me improve my craft. Another big thank-you goes to Alexa Donne for starting the program and to all of my fellow mentees and mentors who I've gotten to know over the past several years.

Fellow Roaring 20s, thanks for providing support during the lead-up to publication.

In researching the knuckleball, the *Knuckleball!* documentary directed by Ricki Stern and Annie Sundberg was helpful and inspiring. I very much recommend *Knuckleball!*

to anyone who is curious about baseball's weirdest pitch and the people who've mastered it. Baseball fans may recognize pieces of Tim Wakefield's and R. A. Dickey's careers in VJ's story. I intended these similarities as a tribute to these remarkable pitchers.

Finally, I'd like to thank every single reader. Thanks for spending time with Vivy.

TURN THE PAGE TO READ
THE FIRST CHAPTER OF
ANOTHER SARAH KAPIT BOOK!

Lara and Caroline Finkel do everything together—until Lara starts a brand-new detective agency, FIASCCO, without Caroline, and Caroline makes a new friend without Lara. But as FIASCCO and the Finkel family mysteries spin out of control, can Caroline and Lara find a way to be friends again?

CHAPTER ONE:

IN WHICH A NEW BUSINESS IS FOUNDED

DO YOU HAVE A MYSTERY THAT NEEDS SOLVING?

Finkel Investigative Agency Solving Consequential
Crimes Only (FIASCCO) is here to help!

Our team of experienced detectives can solve all/most
mysteries, including theft, missing pets, and other matters
requiring detecting skill and general awesomeness.

For more information, talk to Lara Finkel ASAP.

NOTE: FIASCCO cannot help find murderers. If you or someone
you know has been murdered, please call the police.

Lara looked over her flyer with a great big frown. It really was too bad she couldn't come up with a name that spelled out FIASCO instead of FIASCCO. She was an excellent speller, in addition to being an excellent investigator. She didn't want anyone to get the wrong idea about that. But it was too late now to change the name. Her parents had not been pleased with her printing so many copies of her flyer using the family printer, and they'd clearly stated that there would be no second edition. So Lara would just have to live with FIASCCO.

Her mother had also insisted that Lara add in the part about not solving murders. At first she'd resisted. After all, Georgia Ketteridge, Girl Super-Detective, would never turn down a murder case if she were lucky enough to find one. But given Lara's unfortunate tendency to get nauseous whenever she saw even a drop of blood, maybe Ima had a point.

Okay, so Lara wouldn't be solving murder cases straight off. So what? She felt completely, totally, 100 percent certain that detective work was going to be her thing. Her cousin Aviva had math, and her sister Caroline had art, and her brother Benny had science-y things. Now, Lara would have detecting. Which just so happened to be way cooler than any of those other things. After having read all four books in the Georgia Ketteridge series, Lara knew she could solve a real-life mystery. If only one would come to her.

It'll come, Lara told herself. The flyers were just step one.

With her mission in mind, Lara gathered up the stack of flyers and headed for the door. It was still only the early afternoon, leaving plenty of time to redecorate the neighborhood in blazing yellow flyers—not Lara's favorite color, but good for getting attention. Hopefully.

For a moment Lara considered enlisting Caroline's help in the matter. As annoying as her little sister could be (very!), Caroline usually made things more fun. She should get Caroline. Yet something inside her rebelled at the idea. Maybe Caroline was her very favorite sibling, separated by a mere fifteen months, but did that mean they had to do absolutely everything together?

No, Lara decided. It did not.

Lara paused when she reached the kitchen. Based on the too-loud talk and enticing vanilla scent, she deduced two things. First, her sister and cousin were in there. Second, they were baking cupcakes. Without her.

Stupid show-off Aviva and her stupid show-off cupcakes. As if it wasn't enough that her cousin moved in last year and immediately became the smartest kid in Lara's grade. Apparently, she also had to bake cupcakes several times a week. They were good cupcakes, too. Lara supposed that was one reason why her sister and brothers failed to recognize the fact that Aviva was actually annoying.

Lara couldn't help it. She marched into the kitchen.

"Hello, Lara," her cousin said, not looking up from her mixing bowl. "We've already put the cupcakes in the oven. But you can still decorate them with us if you want."

"Pretty please? It will be fun," Caroline said. She spoke

using a computer voice that came out of her tablet. That was how Caroline talked. She'd type things into an app, and then a voice from her tablet—a snotty-sounding British lady—would speak her words out loud.

"No," Lara said firmly. Detective business required her full attention.

She was about to leave Caroline and Aviva for good when her older brother Noah walked in.

"Hello annoying sisters," he said.. "And not-at-all annoying cousin who makes excellent baked goods."

Lara stuck her tongue out at him and straightened her stack of flyers.

"I helped with the cupcakes, so you might want to reconsider what you just said," Caroline said.

"In that case, I take it back until I've got my cupcakes. At least for you, Lina-Lin." Noah gave his cheekiest smile. His eyes fell on Lara's stack of flyers. "Huh. What do you have there, Lara?"

Noah snatched a flyer without asking. As he read, Lara chewed on her lip. It's not like she needed Noah's permission for anything. Of course she didn't. Still, she cared what her brother thought. A lot.

"Um. How are you an experienced detective?" Noah asked.

Lara scowled. Rude!

"I found Benny's favorite toy car for him last week, after everyone else gave up on it," she informed her brother. "Plus I figured out the cause of Kugel's hairball problem. It was the kettle corn he kept sneaking in the middle of the night."

"So you're going from hairball investigations to solving actual mysteries?"

A snicker came from Aviva's corner of the room. Lara forced herself to stay focused. Aviva's opinions did not matter in the slightest.

"Absolutely," Lara said. "The Mystery of the Hairball was very difficult to crack. And now Kugel hasn't had a single hairball in two weeks thanks to me."

"That is a true miracle."

"Yes, it is," Lara said, nobly choosing to ignore Noah's sarcasm.

Fists clenched, Lara reminded herself that Georgia Ketteridge was graceful even when dealing with annoying people.

"Why are you calling it *F-I-A-S-C-C-O*?" he asked.

"Because it sounds good. Any new business needs a marketing plan."

"Sure," Noah said in his I'm-going-to-tell-you-what-you-want-to-hear-but-I-don't-really-mean-it voice. Lara despised that voice. "Um, you do know what *fiasco* means, right?"

Lara snatched the flyer out of Noah's hands. "Of course I do."

"Then why did you name your detective agency after it?"

"Well, the idea is that when you have a fiasco, you go to FIASCCO. Get it?"

"Not really," Noah muttered.

"It does not make sense to me, either," Aviva said. As if anyone had asked her!

That was quite enough. Noah and Aviva just didn't understand. Unfortunate, certainly, but it's not like Lara actually needed help from them. Or anyone else. She straightened her pile of flyers and gave everyone a properly disdainful look. Well, at least she hoped it showed proper disdain.

"I am going to post these around. If anyone you know needs mystery-solving services, I'm here to help," she said.

And she marched out of the house clutching her flyers.

It took more than an hour, but every house on the block got a FIASCCO flyer. With every paper she placed on a doorstep, hope swelled in Lara's chest. True, she didn't know if anyone on the street needed a detective. But surely someone out of all these people would want to hire her.

As she went from door to door, Lara allowed her mind to wander. She had heard—many, many times—that people on the autism spectrum were blessed with extraordinary abilities. But she couldn't help but think that somehow this particular trait had passed her by.

Once she'd said as much to Ima, who responded with a sigh. "You're a fast reader," her mother pointed out. "And you remember what you read perfectly."

"Only because I read my books so many times!"

Lara loved books as though they were dear friends. In her experience, they were certainly more reliable than people-friends. But honestly, what kind of a special talent was *reading*? Ima didn't get it at all.

"And you're good at writing, too," Ima had continued. "All of your teachers praise your essays."

There wasn't much point in saying that writing essays was a rather unimpressive talent. Ima would only protest. Even though it was totally and completely true.

After all, Lara reasoned, they didn't put essays up next to the great paintings in museums. Nobody had ever written a newspaper article about a particularly skilled essay-writer. Kids at school never told her "Great essay! Can you show me how to do that?" the way people did with Caroline's drawings.

Detective work was different. Once she succeeded with that, she would be special, too.

For a moment, Lara wondered if flyers were perhaps not the preferred method for finding mysteries. In the Georgia Ketteridge books, mysteries just appeared. Georgia's uncle once fell victim to an attempted robbery. But Lara couldn't count on that kind of luck.

As she marched back to her house, Lara's mind burst with thoughts of her detective agency. She felt confident—well, mostly confident—that she could find a mystery before school started up again in a few weeks. After that, maybe there would be school-related mysteries for her to solve. And then? Why, she'd practically be an established detective.

She even had her very own detective notebook. True, it was just a black-and-white composition notebook that said "FIASCCO" on the front, but still. It counted.

"What are you doing?" a voice asked.

Lara spun around to find Caroline, who was wearing her special harness and straps. It helped her lug around her tablet without tiring out her arms too much.

Caroline's computer voice always spoke in the same flat tone. Still, Lara could swear that her sister sounded extra whiny.

"Oh, I was just delivering flyers for my new detective agency," Lara said. Her chest swelled at the word *my*.

"Can I help?"

"No!" Lara said immediately. The look on Caroline's face made her stomach squirm. "I mean, I'm almost done. So you can't. Sorry."

That ought to do it, she thought. Caroline couldn't possibly stay upset for long. Right?

"Why didn't you ask me to help?" her sister asked. After she finished typing she looked expectantly at Lara.

Lara should make up some excuse about having forgotten to ask. Caroline would believe her. Probably. But when she opened her mouth to invent something that sounded believable, entirely different words came out. "I didn't need your help."

Big mistake. Caroline tapped away at her tablet, her jaw clenched firmly. Lara bounced on her toes while she waited for her sister to finish typing.

"I would be good at being a detective," Caroline said finally. "I would."

Lara blinked. She had not considered whether or not

her sister would be good at detecting. That wasn't the point. The whole point of FIASCCO was that she, Lara Finkel, was going to be a detective. Caroline already had her special thing!

Gulping in a deep breath, Lara prepared herself to say something wise and sisterly. Something that would magically make Caroline understand why she absolutely could not be a part of FIASCCO.

Instead, Lara said, "Are you absolutely sure about that? There's a lot that goes into being a detective, you know."

The moment the words escaped her mouth Lara realized her mistake. Caroline tore her eyes away from the screen and delivered a glare that made Lara's ankles shake. It really was remarkable how her eleven-year-old sister could imitate their mother so precisely.

"Just because I can't talk doesn't mean that I can't be a detective, Lara."

As always, Caroline's computer voice did not waver. She might as well have been reciting state capitals. Or commenting on the rather large number of trees in Seattle. But Lara knew her sister was capital-U Upset. She knew it from the tightness of Caroline's jaw and the clenched fist flapping by her side.

"I never said you can't be a detective." Lara did her best

to imitate the tablet's calm monotone, but a squeak crept into her voice. "I just said you couldn't be in FIASCCO."

Logically, Lara knew that such a distinction was unlikely to satisfy her sister. Yet it was true. If Caroline couldn't see that, it wasn't Lara's problem.

Caroline glared at Lara's stack of flyers as though it reeked of Kugel's litter box contents. Her fingers danced across the screen at top speed, and Lara didn't have to wait very long at all to hear her response.

"Fine. Be that way. By the way, 'fiasco' is a stupid name."

And with that, Caroline closed her tablet shut and marched back toward the house. As Lara watched Caroline disappear behind the bright yellow door, she chewed on the edges of her lip.

For a moment, Lara considered going after her sister and begging for forgiveness. She made it three whole steps before drawing to a stop.

Lara wasn't going to apologize for starting her own detective agency. After all, it wasn't like Caroline did absolutely everything with her. Lara thought of the many occasions when she'd walked in on her sister doing something with Aviva. Like baking cupcakes, for example. Caroline hadn't apologized to Lara for the fact that she apparently preferred to spend time in the company of the world's most annoying cousin. Why should Lara apologize for FIASCCO?

Feeling satisfied with her decision to not apologize for anything, Lara posted the final FIASCCO flyer on a large tree in the Finkels' front yard.

Just as she was admiring her work, her father very rudely interrupted. From his place in the parked car, he tapped up against the car window. Lara jumped. "Lara-bear!" he said. "Get in the car. I need you and your sister for some things."

"What things?" she asked crossly.

"Consider it adventuring of the errands variety," Dad replied.

That was not promising. Lara groaned, but she marched over and got into her father's car. When she glanced out the window and spotted her flyer, she couldn't help but smile. flyer FIASCCO would succeed. She felt sure of it.

A moment later, Caroline entered the car. She did not say anything to Lara. She didn't even bother keeping her speech app open, but instead started playing Candy Crush.

Fine. It's not like Lara actually needed her sister.